The Sleep of Baby Filbertson

And other stories

James Leo Herlihy
RosettaBooks®

Cover jacket design by Christian Fuenfhausen
ISBN (paperback): 978-0-7953-5141-9
ISBN (e-Pub): 978-0-7953-5120-4

For Anaïs

Also Available
By James Leo Herlihy

CONTENTS

"...In the fall one walks in the orchards and the ground is hard with frost underfoot...On the trees are only a few gnarled apples that the pickers have rejected...One nibbles at them and they are delicious. Into a little round place at the side of the apple has been gathered all of its sweetness. One runs from tree to tree over the frosted ground picking the gnarled, twisted apples and filling his pockets with them. Only the few know the sweetness of the twisted apples."

SHERWOOD ANDERSON
in *Winesburg, Ohio*

The Sleep of Baby Filbertson

Rudy was awake now but his body had not changed from its position of sleep. Under the sheet he lay coiled like a serpent, his knees and elbows and his face all nestled in a fat and private circle. His mother stood at his bedside.

"Baby Filbertson, I'm tired and I'm mad. It's two o'clock in the afternoon. Dammit, I said P.M. Tell *me* you never dipped into my phenobarbitals last night!"

He answered without moving: "Mother, I swear hand on the Bible, if I touched one pheeny in this house last night, God strike me dead an' you along with me!"

"Leave me the hell out of it, brother," she said.

"Anyway I'm sick," Rudy said, "somethin' wrong with m'head."

"You think your head's in bad shape *now*..." She held up the back of her hand and threatened his face with it. "Groggy from stolen phenobarbs is your trouble."

"I already swore on the Bible may I be struck dead," he said, still without moving. "I wasn't struck, was I?"

"Show me somebody sleeps fourteen hours 'thout a pill and brother, I'll show you a cock-eyed snake-in-the-grass wouldn' know the truth 'f he got hit on his head with it." She closed her fat hand over the corner of the sheet and ripped it from the bed. "Git up!"

Rudy rolled over on his back and covered his private section with the pillow. Then he looked up at his mother who stood with arms akimbo, smoke pouring from her nostrils, and an inch of cigarette hanging from her lips, grinning like a nasty cartoon bulldog. Rudy sat up: "You're a sonofabitch," he said.

Her hand landed with great force and speed on the side of his face. Rudy screamed as his head struck the mattress.

"Make me sick," she said, waddling out of the room, her bedroom slippers going whoosh-slap whoosh-slap under her like the fins of some walking dream-fish. "Nineteen years old, I think he's still in di'pers." The door slammed shut.

Rudy lay looking at his body, the breasts as full as a young girl's; below them, a larger more distant hill of stomach and near the foot of the bed, two groups of toes like uncooked sausages pointed vaguely toward the ceiling. Rudy was good and damned fed up. Trying to get one puny little sleeping capsule from her was like sticking up the First National Bank. He had a good notion just to pack up a few things, including enough money to get as far as Hollywood, and just leave her there in the middle of New York to shift for herself. And, brother, when it came to that, she knew how to shift. She got *her* sleeping pills, didn't she? You bet your bottom dollar she got hers. And enough money to last for life, too: had his father certified mentally non-something-or-other and locked up at Belle Grove (not that the skunk didn't deserve it), then went to court and had the separation made legal, tied up half of the old cuss's money in a trust fund so she could give up day nursing and sit on her fat tail for life without twitching a muscle she didn't want to twitch. Except the one under her left eye. That'd probably be twitching from now on. Doctor called it nerves.

Maybe he'd go away alone, to anywhere, even if it was back to New Orleans, then get himself a job though Lord knew where: perhaps a loan office could use him for evaluating pearls, or the movies in funny fat person parts, or maybe he'd brush up on his piano and take voice, if they ever stayed in one place long enough, and get himself a job singing and playing in a saloon. Eventually, of course, Rudy knew he'd end up in Hollywood.

He could hear the whoosh-slap of her slippers approaching on the other side of the door. He got out of bed and stepped into his trousers. She opened the door and stood watching him.

"If you ain't a sight," she said. "Gain another pound, you be a *real* hog, that's for damn sure!"

"'Bout like you, Mother?" he said. "That's what I'm aimin' for."

"Yeah, 'bout like me, son. Titties an' all."

The ironing board was set up in the main room of the apartment. There were three altogether: two bedrooms and this main room which was used for everything but sleeping and bathing. In an alcove near the bathroom door stood a cream-coloured refrigerator on which a previous tenant had glued a picture of a yellow swan eating a pink water lily. Rudy opened the door. Inside were four bottles of Coca-Cola, half a melon, a bottle of chocolate milk and a pound of bacon. He took one of the Coca-Colas and the melon, sat on the couch, turned on the radio and began to eat.

Daisy Filbertson held the iron upside down under her face. "If you wasn't so soft in the head you'd get you a nylon shirt, don't need pressin'." She spat on the iron; it sizzled. "Listen t'me, Baby Filbertson, turn off that damn radio, your mother's talkin'. I know you don't give one lovely hoot if I iron from now till hell won't have it, but I do brother. *Turn that damn thing off!*"

Rudy was listening to a radio commercial paid for by a correspondence school that taught Spanish in six weeks. Maybe he'd slip away to Trinidad and become a calypso singer.

" ...don't leave it sit there," Daisy was saying as the commercial gave place to a song called "Give Me a Kiss to Build a Dream on". "Put that rind in the pail and take it all down t' the street. Been bad pork in there since last night, startin' t' smell."

The entire island seemed to have been submerged in an ocean of hot light and walking through it required a swimmer's effort. Women invented parasols made of newspapers to blind them from the sun, and men blotted their foreheads with handkerchiefs and squirmed inside their suits. Yet it seemed to Rudy more bearable on the street than it had been inside where Daisy's ironing sent the temperature even higher.

He wandered down Broadway and after only a few blocks he was tired. He went into the subway station at 72nd Street, stuck a dime in the slot, pushed through the turnstile and descended the stairway into an airless chamber illuminated by naked light bulbs. Several people stood about, with the unhappy but patient air of travellers to Hell who realize the journey is inevitable, waiting for the Seventh Avenue Local.

When the train arrived, Rudy boarded the last car. He stood at the rear and looked out the window, and then he watched the station platform grow smaller and smaller as he and the train were drawn deeper and deeper with greater and greater speed into the tunnel. It was like that quick and sensuous falling into sleep on a night when he'd stolen one of the magic pheenies. Occasional shafts of sudden light dropped from gratings in the street above and made flaws in the blackness.

Now ordinarily he'd go to bed and the dreams took him right smack back to Louisiana where there was nothing but trouble; night before last he'd barely closed his eyes but what he found himself going through that car accident all over again. Started out by driving down Jackson Street, turned the corner into Chinaberry Avenue, got to looking at that same coon leaning on the lamp-post, and just like it was happening all over again only this time faster, forgot to straighten up in time and there he was parked on the sidewalk with the car buried up to its windshield in Hodgeson's furniture store, and the same fat policeman lying flat on his back on one of the display beds in the window, his right leg bleeding like a live pig stuck through the middle with a barbecue sword.

Every time he dreamed it, Rudy'd wake up laughing— also just as it'd really happened: sat there laughing like a fool hyena and made the policeman all the madder—but in his dreaming the laughing hurt him some, like it was his own leg bleeding. And then all day long he'd see, as if through a window in his mind, way off somewhere, that coloured boy leaning on the lamp-post like he was holding up the world.

Rudy did not want to think about the people of his dreams but they often visited his mind uninvited. The principal figure was the young Negro. Rudy would always see, as if tattooed in pink on the man's brown neck, a long sickle-shaped scar which stretched from his left ear to his Adam's apple and then descended down the length of his throat. His eyes were kind and warm but in the kindness itself, Rudy sensed some terrible store of violent energy that attracted him at the same moment that it repelled him. Rudy could not imagine the nature of the harm this kind-eyed Negro's dark and unfathomable cunning would one day inflict upon him. Nor could he remember any longer whether the Negro on the street corner looked like the person he knew from dreaming, or if his identifying marks, the eyes and the pink scar, had been placed there by that other dark and unknown stranger, the artisan who designed the dreams.

The train came to a stop at 50th Street. Rudy climbed out of the subway pit, his energy by now at a low ebb. He hated New York for its heat and for its concrete that sustained the heat even through the night all summer long, and his mother for her strange restlessness that had brought them here several weeks ago.

It was her often-stated intention, now that she had achieved a degree of economic freedom from her husband whom she hated, to see the world. But Rudy could not understand why it was that each time they arrived in some new city—San Francisco, Santa Fe, Chicago, and now New York—she would install herself like a hibernating bear in some unpleasant cave and refuse to move outside the door. It made their travelling absurd and their lives pointless. On the journey itself she would fill herself with phenobarbital and seldom looked out the train window, except perhaps to discern whether it was night or day. After they had been in a city for several weeks or months, he might come home at almost any moment to find that, without warning or even a hint of any kind, she had packed their bags and had engaged space for them on a train or a bus to some new destination.

"Seen enough o' this damn town," she'd said on the afternoon they'd left San Francisco. "Get your face washed, Baby, we got a train to catch at four-thirty."

"Seen *enough* of it!" Rudy had said. "Seen nothin' of it's the fact of the matter!"

"Lousy cotton-pickin' fog!" she grumbled. "Come on, get your shirt on!" Rudy remembered that in Santa Fe there'd been too much cotton-pickin' sunshine and in Chicago the factory smoke; it was yet to be learned which aspect of New York she would find too damn cotton-pickin'.

During their first days here she had said at least six different times: "Goin' out Monday morning t'see that dame with the torch in New York Harbour, providin' the weather's decent." But when the weather had been decent a backache had stopped her, or she'd had to stick around the place as she was expecting some imaginary telegram.

It was as if Daisy had reached a point in her living at which she suspected that life held no further promise, and rather than to risk finding this true, she went through it grumbling, complaining, partially hypnotized by sleeping capsules, her unconscious mind artfully avoiding direct contact with whatever remained to be experienced.

Now, from the top of the subway steps, Rudy could see the marquee of the Roxy Theatre. It was featuring a Ginger Rogers picture and on its stage was an ice show. He bought a ticket and went inside: the temperature was thirty degrees cooler; a girl with yellow hair sold him a package of Life Savers; ushers stood like palace guards at a dozen inner doors; on either side of the stage, high in the theatre's lofts, were golden stairways that led to no one knew what secret chambers, and covering it all like the ceiling of heaven itself, were delicate designs carved in wood and lighted by dim hidden sources; on the screen Miss Rogers was seated at a cocktail bar quarrelling with an elderly gentleman.

But Rudy's mind was never quite so taken up with what happened on the screen as with what might be happening instead if he were playing a particular role himself and could follow random impulses and take the story in directions more to his own choosing. Now and then the entrance of a beautiful person required some quick revision of the plot, or the music under the story would speak out some fevered crescendo that brought his dreaming to a new beginning. And in this way, the hottest hours of Rudy's afternoon passed.

Finally, the ice show came to an end. The magnificent curtains descended like the skirts of a mammoth goddess from between the golden stairways. A swift march began to play as the people left their seats and pushed their way up the aisles, fighting those now coming in. In the back of Rudy's neck was that cotton-candy ache that comes of looking too long at too many bonbon colours of changing lights and glitter-spangled costumes. His eyes ached and he was hungry.

He wandered, somewhat dizzy, into the daylight. By the time he reached the sidewalk his hunger had grown almost to pain. He walked west on 50th Street in search of hot dogs but before he reached a restaurant some sweet aroma gripped his nose like a claw and drew him into a shop where a dozen varieties of popped corn and nuts had been dipped in a golden liquid candy.

He bought a bag of caramel corn and returned to the street; the first mouthful was delicious, but at the moment it reached his stomach he began to feel ill. Rudy could never understand this chemistry of pleasure, the way it seemed that all sweetness was in reality a poison. But the hunger drove him to take another mouthful, and then a third.

All at once a police whistle shrieked, an automobile sounded in his ear, a woman's voice said: watch out mister! and Rudy felt a sudden heavy push in his stomach. Then he was lying on his back in the street, surrounded by a steadily growing crowd.

"Here's the driver of the car," said a woman's voice.

"You hurt, kid?" a man asked.

Rudy's right hand was bruised where he had tried to break his fall, and in his left, as if it had been the widow's baby snatched in the nick of time from the burning house, he clutched the white sack of caramel corn. He was not seriously hurt and he knew it. More than anything else he felt humiliated and foolish. "Why don't everybody go away and leave me alone?"

The man who had driven the car helped Rudy to his feet.

"You hurt?"

"No, I ain't hurt; just get back in your damn car and drive away."

A woman's voice behind Rudy said: "It was your fault, sonny, you walked right into him."

"You want me to take you home, kid?" the driver asked.

Rudy felt caged in by the crowd. He moved sullenly to the sidewalk. "I'm not hurt for Chrissake, lea' me alone."

He tried to walk as if nothing were wrong, but his bruised knee caused him to limp. He was less than half a block away when he could see from the corner of his eye someone following him. This irritated him and he began to walk faster.

One night he had dreamed he was walking down Chinaberry Avenue with a parasol over his head—stark naked! He felt like that now. The young man behind him ran to catch up with Rudy. He was a Negro, tall, copper-skinned, athletic, probably somewhere in his twenties. "You want me to get you a taxi?" he said, "there's something wrong with your foot."

His first impulse was to send the stranger away, but when Rudy frowned and looked into the man's face, the smile he found there was so kind and warm that he was instantly disarmed by it. In the Negro's manner was some deeply appealing intimacy, the unequivocal sympathy of an animal. It was as if a pair of invisible arms, brown and strong as an animal's, had reached out and surrounded him to protect him from the eyes of the street, and to soothe his hurts for which he suddenly felt no shame.

The young Negro called a taxi. He opened the door and Rudy climbed in. "I think you better go right on up to a doctor," the Negro said. Rudy watched as the young man closed the cab door.

"Won't you get in and ride uptown with me?" Rudy said. The stranger smiled and shook his head. "Naw. I'll just catch a bus."

As the Negro turned to walk away, Rudy was suddenly gripped with panic. "Hey, wait a minute!" he said. When the young man returned to the taxi and lowered his head through the window, Rudy could find nothing to say. But the thought of being separated from the stranger terrified him. "I don't even know your name," he said finally. The other man thrust his hand through the open window: "I'm Clyde," he said, "Clyde Williams."

Rudy took Clyde's hand in both of his and held it tightly. "My name's Rudy. I want you to ride with me, hear? Come on, Clyde, please!"

Clyde continued to smile but a frown settled into his face between his eyebrows: "You got money enough to pay the cab?"

Rudy said he had.

"Well, you're all right then, Rudy; you just tell the fella where you want to go, and he'll take you there. Everything's going to be all right. I'll see you some more, Rudy."

Clyde withdrew his hand from Rudy's. The frown left his face, he smiled broadly, waved his hand and walked away. The taxi started to move. Rudy moved forward on to one of the small folding seats and stuck his face out the window. As the cab reached the corner, Rudy saw Clyde again. He was waiting for a bus and, as he waited, he leaned on a lamp-post.

The traffic light was green and the driver placed the gears into second position and withdrew his foot. As the car moved more rapidly forward, Rudy was able to get a last good look at his friend. He was certain that he could discern, on Clyde's neck, glistening from his ear to his throat and disappearing down into his shirt, a scar which was like a sickle tattooed in pink.

Rudy got out of the cab in front of his apartment house. He paid the driver and walked slowly up the steps to the third floor. He was no longer aware of the pain in his leg.

Daisy was lying on the couch with her eyes closed, her glasses on, a small cigarette butt protruding from her lips. When Rudy closed the door, her eyes popped open.

"Where you been, brother?"

Rudy flopped into a chair and said nothing. The muscle under Daisy's left eye began to twitch as she came more fully awake. "Baby Filbertson, I said where you been?" Rudy slowly drew his pantleg up past his knee, baring a red bruise the size of a quarter.

"Well!" Daisy said. "Twinkletoes fell on his ass!" She went into the bathroom and returned with a first-aid kit. "It's iodine and it's gonna hurt, so keep your mouth shut." Then she painted the wound liberally and when she had finished the edges were a deep orange. "Didn't flinch, did he? I believe m'soul he's turnin' into a man! Now what happened?"

Rudy was slumped deep into the chair, it contained him like giant arms. "Like t'got killed is all," he said. "Damn Greyhound bus come tear-assin' around 50th Street corner o' Broadway. I'd got squashed good haddin been for some coon shoved me outa the way, nick o' time. Anyway, fell on m'knees."

"You let a nigger shove you on the sidewalk?"

"Yeah. I let'im. Saved m'neck. You talk like a damn fool!"

Daisy went to the stove which was above the refrigerator and boiled some spaghetti. She opened a can of tomato soup and poured that over the top of it. Then she fried several strips of bacon. Daisy and Rudy ate their dinners in irritated silence. Then Daisy returned to the couch. She switched the radio on and began to thumb through a paper-backed detective novel.

Rudy went to his room. The air was still moist and warm even though the sun was gone. He removed his clothes and lay on the bed. In his mind he reproached himself for the way he had mishandled the events of the day. Should've got out of that damn taxicab right there'n' then, he thought; should've walked right over to that one called hisself Clyde Williams and said to him: Boy, who the hell're you, followin' me all the way up here from Lousiana, could swear I seen you in N'Orleans, Shreveport, Santa Fe, and Lord knows how many dreams you poked your black nose into. Should've had it right out with him there'n'then, make an end to it one way or the other.

Rudy went through this dialogue in his mind several times until he had memorized it, and through several variations of the same words in which he tried to improve on the original, and soon he was in a light sleep, a haunted ordinary non-pheeny sleep in which all the dreams were wild, terrible, filled with blazing technicolour violence: He was the captive of a band of dark-skinned gypsies who had taken him into a southern wood where they had built a large fire and tied him to a tree alongside of it. Then like black magicians or voodoo madmen they danced and mumbled and shrieked grinning curses to an unbearable thump-thump-*thump* drumbeat which seemed to go on for a hundred days and nights. They had removed all of

Rudy's clothes and, tied to the tree by the stifling heat of the fire, the perspiration fell like blood from his body, and caused itches impossible to scratch.

Suddenly there was complete silence. The gypsies sat by the fireside with brilliant savage-toothed grins fixed on their faces as if painted there. A fat gypsy squaw appeared before Rudy and stood so close to him he could smell her sour air on his face. Her eyes held his in a kind of hypnotic trance for a long moment and then, with a movement so quick he could not follow it with his eyes, she had withdrawn, from under her great shawl, a shining silver-bladed breadknife; with her free hand she took hold of his sex and with the knife she severed it from his body and threw it into the fire. Rudy was instantly released from the tree. He was handed a small pink parasol and ordered to dance.

Then there was a loud tapping sound that seemed to be made by the contact of a man's knuckles on a pane of glass.

This noise awakened him and the dream ended. Rudy sat up and looked about the room. But no one was there. After the raucousness of the dream, the entire world seemed to be in a state of iced silence. The table lamp issued a shrill white light that made the bedsheets look like icebergs gleaming under moonlight. The articles on the bureau seemed fragile, useless, as if they had been dried up while he slept and covered by invisible dust like objects in a museum which, once removed from their glass cases or unglued from their mountings, might crumble like sculptures in sand.

There was no accounting for this strangeness that had settled on the world. He wanted desperately to get away from it, perhaps into a pheeny sleep in some country so far away that when he woke he would never remember where he'd been, some deep dark warm sleep from which he would wake in some other place, a new and quiet land not on this earth.

Once more he heard the noise that had caused his dream to end. He was certain that someone was knocking on his bedroom window. He remained in bed, transfixed, chilled with fear, eyes on the window, listening. Now he could hear a voice calling to him: Rudy, let me in Rudy, I won't hurt you, Rudy, I'm your friend.

Rudy was no longer afraid. When Clyde's face appeared at the window, he recognized it instantly, and the long sickle-shaped scar as well. "Clyde, what you want?" he said. "What's the idea followin' me all over hell'n' back, and now come scarin' me like this, the middle of the night. You crazy?" But he no longer felt impelled to reproach Clyde. It was as if they had been friends for a long time and once again, as on the street in the afternoon, Rudy trusted the warm animal eyes, and he could feel the brown strength of invisible arms reaching out, surrounding him to protect him. He heard Clyde's voice again: "Rudy, let me in. Please let me in."

"Wait a second, you black idiot," Rudy said, gently mocking his friend. "Wait'll I get m'drawers on." He scrambled into his trousers. Inside of him there was excitement, happiness.

By placing his foot on the steam radiator, Rudy was able to hoist himself up to the window-sill where he sat and looked out. The ground was three storeys below. There was no fire escape anywhere and the small concrete garden was empty. Rudy called from the window: "Clyde, Clyde! Where in hell did you go, you sonofabitch. Come back here."

Across the courtyard, a woman stood in a window. But no one else could be seen. A tall elm that grew out of the concrete garden stood perfectly still. The woman in the window watched Rudy. "Hey mister," she said in a loud stage whisper: "Pipe down will you. We got sickness here."

Climbing back into his room, Rudy's foot slipped from the radiator. He fell to the floor and landed once again on his hands and knees. The irritation of his early bruises angered him. He sat on the floor cursing and grumbling at first to himself, then gradually louder and louder. Everything seemed to have been conspiring for his annoyance: the heat which brought perspiration from his pores to roll down and cover that which had dried on his body while he slept; Clyde, who probably at this very moment sat crosslegged on the roof, laughing at him, and his mother who dragged him with her from city to city and never would stay in one place long enough for him to get a start on his voice lessons—she didn't care if he never got to Hollywood; the truth was that no one cared a good cotton-picking goddam for him, there it was, the fact of the matter right on the line—and he began to weep.

He leaned his head on the bed. The sheet felt mercifully cool against his cheek. He stopped crying for a moment to look longingly at that endless desert of icebergs made by the rumpled sheet. They were like the lifeless mountains and valleys one might find on a planet such as the moon was thought to be.

He drew himself to his feet and left his room in search of the sleeping capsules. He looked on the floor of the closets, behind the stacks of magazines on the mantelpiece, in all of the strange unlikely places his mother might think of, even back behind the cushions on the davenport and in a box of shredded wheat on the kitchen shelf. He knew she had them stashed away all over the apartment. Last night he'd found a bottle of them in an old shoe away under a pile of laundry on the bathroom floor and another believe it or not buried in a box of sanitary napkins on top of the toilet.

Several minutes later Rudy found himself digging with his bare hands into the depths of the garbage pail.

Finally, with the courage of utter desperation, silent as a burglar, Rudy turned the door knob and eased open the door of his mother's bedroom.

She was snoring. The room was partly illuminated by moonlight. He could see Daisy's face. The light shone on her moist eyelids and they glistened like false eyes. A bottle of capsules stood on the small table next to the head of her bed. Rudy crept slowly toward them, slowly, taking care to set his weight down a little at a time in order to test the strength of the boards: the weak ones were sure to creak.

He reached the side of her bed. Daisy's snoring continued. He stood stock-still, taking one long moment just to look at her. Her nightgown was torn and one of her breasts was revealed. It seemed limp and liquid as if its shape depended entirely upon gravity; the large brown nipple gaped blindly at the ceiling. It was just possible she'd be playing possum, waiting to catch him in the act. No, it was a real sleep. Her breathing was slow and noisy, her eye did not twitch at all as it would if she were awake.

Rudy had just put his arm forward, toward the table, when Daisy's hand sprang forward and gripped his wrist like a claw. Her eyes snapped open at the same instant. Rudy jumped back and cried out, and his heart was beating fast. At the same moment, he could not help admiring her speed.

"Caught ya damn sneak thief," she said, glowering at him, her hand still fixed bear-like on his wrist.

"Let go, dammit, you're hurtin' me."

"I've heard tell o' people that kill sneak thieves in the night kill 'em dead as hell!" she said.

"You'd laugh out o' the other end, 'f I was to have a heart attack cause o' you."

"Attack ahead, Filbertson; g'on, turn blue! Could'n' care less."

"I should've snuk in here 'th a breadknife 'n' stuck it in yer gizzard. Better keep on sleepin' like a sly damned old fox, or one o' these days I'm apt to."

Her eyes glared through the dark at him like false eyes with some nightmare knowledge frozen dead inside of them: "Brother, where you're headin' there won't be any breadknife left lyin' around."

Rudy's heart continued to beat too rapidly and the palms of his hands and the arches of his feet were moist and hot. His breath came in short nervous gasps and in his mind were the ghosts of a hundred or more dark-skinned gypsies. His mother's eyes were steady and cold as they penetrated his mind. Then a small grin disfigured her mouth, and her eye began to twitch.

"Mother," Rudy said in a sad voice that was almost a whimper, "can I have a pheeny?"

"One" she said.

He took a capsule from the bottle and replaced the lid.

"Thanks. M'damned head hurts."

He turned quickly and left the room. When he reached the bathroom, he could hear her calling to him: "Baby Filbertson! Baby Filbertson!" He drew a glass of cool water from the tap. She was still calling to him as he swallowed the capsule. "Baby Filbertson, come kiss your mother good night." But he pretended not to hear. He hurried to his bedroom and turned out the light. "Baby Filbertson," she called. Her voice was heavy and angry and it filled the house like an air-raid siren in a doomed city. "Come kiss your mother, goddamit! Hear now?"

She could go to hell, he thought. Clyde was probably still seated on the roof, his head and shoulders silhouetted against the sky. He could go to hell too.

Rudy believed he could feel the capsule exploding inside of him, soothing him with its thousands of warm hands that massaged gently every vessel of his bloodstream. One pheeny was not very strong, he knew that, but there were many tricks for getting to sleep fast: for instance, arithmetic, get to thinking about figures and pretty soon you drop off.

Ninety years from now, he began, I'll be a hundred and nine. Five years ago I was fourteen and weighed two hundred and eleven pounds. Nine years ago I was ten and weighed a hundred. Fifteen years ago I don't know what I weighed but I was four, and five years before that I wasn't even thought of yet and didn't weigh an ounce.

Imagining himself weightless, even unborn, he was soon fast asleep, wrapped into himself, knees and elbows and head grouped together. A sheet covered him entirely so that his bed was like a slab on which lay the corpse of some giant foetus.

A Summer for the Dead

1

People all through the San Gabriel Valley will remember the summer of 1950: heat, smog and humidity made a hell of all these California cities and many deaths were imputed to it. Those who did not have to remain in the streets took cover behind drawn window shades and fanned themselves with palmetto leaves or old newspapers, their free hands rubbing their smog-burnt eyes; and any bird that had strength enough in him picked up his wings and flew away. After the first day or two an empty stillness settled in and you missed the usual, the expected, the livingness of the world: the haggling of policemen with motorists, noisy games of children, strolling old ladies in pink lace hats, the flights of all those deserting birds. The world had been taken over by a race of strange somnambulists to whom you seldom bothered to nod or even say hello.

Such an extreme in the weather brought complaints from nearly everyone. But there was one young man who believed, at the beginning of the crisis, that this might turn out to be the favourite summer of his life. He lived alone on the top floor of an old rooming house behind the Pasadena Civic Auditorium. Pasadena had been his home for several years and though he had always been fond of it, its clean shaded streets and the rose gardens everywhere, white buildings and the churchlike quiet of the nights, he now found it ideal.

Among the people who knew him, or rather, who were acquainted with him—for no one claimed to *know* Wesley Stuart—there existed various theories to explain his strangeness. Some guessed he was an artist or a poet who had not yet discovered his powers and that his silences were impregnated with lofty thoughts; while at least one person, his landlady, believed he suffered from some terrible spiritual hunger for which she knew a cure; and there were persons less sympathetic to oddness in others and they considered him either stupid or conceited or believed his remoteness to be an affectation.

Late one afternoon, his landlady Mrs. Kromer, a rawboned giant of a woman, was seated spread-legged behind a broad bamboo screen on her front porch. Her flowered cotton housedress clung damp to her; and her feet, long ones with red-knuckled toes, were bare. A pretty young girl sat next to her in a green silk kimono that was torn under one arm. Her name was Faye Zelger.

Wesley had just returned from work and as he walked up the porch steps, Faye and Mrs. Kromer were squeezing lemon juice into their mouths. The old woman's face was so large that any movement in it would attract attention anywhere; the jaw is like a great sac of skin stuffed with a thick round cowbone, a lantern jaw, and whenever she sucks her teeth in church children often crane their necks to watch. Now Wesley paused for a moment to watch her attack on the lemon.

"Somebody claims it's a help," Mrs. Kromer said. "Got another'n if you wanta try it."

The girl winked at Wesley as if inviting him to humour the old woman. "Go ahead, Wes. Get yourself a lemon."

Faye had been brought up in Florida and she spoke with a broad Southern accent. "They work real charms, lemons."

"No thanks, I feel fine. I like it hot."

Faye smiled as she searched about in her mind for an answer. But Wesley did not wait for it. When he had gone inside Faye raised her eyebrows superciliously and turned to Mrs. Kromer. "Loves it," she said. "Thinks it's just glorious. I suppose if we all drop dead, he'll—think that's just glorious, too." She looked at the lemon and shuddered with disgust. "Mr. Tin God. Lord he gives me a stiff pain right where I sit."

"That's puttin' it plain enough," Mrs. Kromer said.

"I'm sorry but I can't stand people that work s'hard to be different'n everybody else."

"You worked up a pretty big smile for him, Missie."

"I admit that. I admit I try to be pleasant to people."

Mrs. Kromer returned to her lemon. "That's nice," she said.

Wesley Stuart had seldom suffered from heat but he had to slow his pace for the third flight of steps and when he entered his room he found it stifling, oppressive.

He removed all of his clothes and since the only other room on the floor had been unrented for several months he walked naked across the hall to the bathroom. He filled the bathtub with cold water and sat down in it. This revived him, he could feel the strength returning to him as if the water in the tub replaced the energy he had lost through his pores. His body was suntanned and he stared at the contrast of his legs with the white of the tub. He flexed the toes of his right foot and watched the ligaments tighten in his ankle and, as he bent his knee, his calf hardened against his thigh. Then he submerged his entire leg and watched the sunbleached hairs float upwards. When he removed his leg from the water these white hairs clung slick to his brown skin and he continued stupidly fascinated with this solitary game of bending and unbending his knee until his back began to ache from it and then he lay down and using his hands as cups poured water all over his head and chest.

When he had dried himself Wesley walked across the hall to his room and lay down on the bed. With the movement of air from the open window and from the skylight in the hall, his room seemed less oppressive to him. Enjoying this comfort, he closed his eyes.

Some minutes later Wesley sat upright in bed and then he heard a shout which must have come from his own throat. Another person was in the room. At the sound of Wesley's voice the man took several steps backward and now he was standing in the doorway.

Suddenly conscious of his own nakedness, Wesley drew the bedspread about his body. There was no way to account for the presence of someone else, uninvited, in his own room. But he had been lying here for some undeterminable length of time and since twilight had already taken place in the city it seemed possible and even likely that this silhouette against the pale column of grey from the skylight might be a figure dreamed up, imagined.

But now as he stared at it, certain features became more distinct: its thick body erect as a sentry, its head thrown back as if listening, the shadow of a stick extending from its hand to the floor. Then it moved. The stick was raised a few inches from the floor and the man rapped it against the frame of the open door. Wesley called out to him but the visitor did not seem to hear. Then Wesley reached toward the ceiling and pulled the string that turned on the light.

In the moment before his eyes became accustomed to the light he cursed and shouted as the man in the doorway stared into the room. Suddenly Wesley was silent. First he had seen the white cane and when his eyes returned to the man's face he realized he was dealing with a blind man. Now he saw a fine white cord extending from a black button in the man's ear. When he could speak, Wesley asked the man what he wanted but the stranger touched the floor with his cane, turned and began to walk slowly down the hall in the direction of the stairs.

Wesley quickly stepped into his trousers and hurried to the door. The man had begun to descend the stairs.

"Hey mister, wait a minute," Wesley said. Then he shouted, "Hey! Wait a minute, will you?"

The man stopped, turned to face Wesley and said, "Somebody talking to me?"

"Yeah. I am. You just knocked on my door. What d'you want?"

"Would you mind talking into this?" He indicated a small square microphone pinned to his shirt. Wesley saw the cord that disappeared under the shirt, reappeared at the collar and connected with the large black earbutton. "I don't hear very well, you have to shout." His voice was low and even, without melody.

Wesley bent down and spoke directly into the microphone: "When you came to my door, I was sleeping. I'm sorry I didn't hear you. Is there anything I can do?"

"I found this card in my door," the blind man said, "and I wanted to ask you to read it to me." Wesley took the card and then he looked at the man's face. He was young, stocky, probably in his late twenties. His skin was ruddy, healthy looking, but it shone with a kind of waxen glaze that seemed unreal. His nose was straight and well shaped with large tensed nostrils, his jaw square and thick, divided in the centre by a deep cleft. He was probably handsome, Wesley thought, but his eyes were disturbing; the almost undefined areas of pale blue faded into the dead whites as if they were the eyes of a badly painted toy doll.

Wesley looked at the card. "It's from the census taker. He wants you to fill it out and drop it in the mail box. Do you live in this building?"

"Since noon. I live in the room across the hall. My name is Earl," He thrust his hand forward. Wesley looked at the extended hand, strong and square, and he noticed that the nails were clean, neatly filed; he stared as if he had never seen a hand before, and then he gripped it with his own and said, "I'm Wesley Stuart."

Then Earl invited him to look at his room. Wesley followed the blind man into the tiny dormer room which he had seen many times before. He knew there was a window at one end, a bed, a dresser and a chair, and nothing more. Earl flipped the light switch but the room remained in darkness. The blind man moved skilfully into the dark and now Wesley could see only his silhouette against the window.

"The bed's hard but I like it that way, you get better rest. And it's got a dresser. See?" Earl moved into a black corner and Wesley could no longer see him at all. "I've got my toilet articles laid out here so I know where to find them. He picked up a large book of perforated cardboard and carried it to the bed. "This is the new *Reader's Digest.* I get it every month."

Wesley, seated on the bed, wondered if he should tell Earl that the light bulb was broken; it seemed strange to be in a room with someone who needed to be told that the light was not burning and even stranger to think that this person's rooms would always be dark. Then, to try blindness for himself, he closed his eyes.

"Are you still here?" Earl said. Listening with his eyes closed, Wesley thought that for Earl all people must simply be voices without bodies. He cupped his hands over his ears and heard a voice from faraway, *"Wesley? Where are you? You still here?"* And it occurred to him that if he refused to answer and if all the people in the world were suddenly blind and deaf he might cease to exist, except inside of himself, a ghost in a dark and silent shell.

"I'm still here," he said. "I'm on the bed." And now his own voice sounded to his covered ears like the voice of another, a stranger outside of himself, or as if his own ghost were whispering to him.

"Why didn't you answer me?" Earl said.

Wesley opened his eyes and rose from the bed. "You better tell Mrs. Kromer to put a new light bulb in here."

"Doesn't it work?"

"No, it doesn't. It's burnt out." Then he excused himself and returned to his apartment. After his experiment in blindness the light shocked his eyes and everything seemed more clearly defined than before: imperfections in the plaster he had never noticed now seemed shabby, the green of the bedspread and the white of the table were startling, almost gaudy.

He opened the refrigerator and found a plate of canned ham and some leftover potato salad. When he had set his table his thoughts turned again to Earl. Wesley was proud of his room and though he realized that the care and imagination with which he had transformed this attic into a splendid apartment would be lost on a visitor who could not see, he knew that Earl who, like all blind people, must be devoted to order, would appreciate the ingenuity with which he had used his space: since the roof of the house was a gabled one there were three alcoves; one of these he used for sleeping, another for cooking and eating, and a third for reading. He went to the door of the room across the hall.

"Earl!"

"Yeah?"

"I wondered if you'd had your dinner?"

"Is it Wesley?"

"Yeah. Have y'eaten yet?"

Earl appeared smiling in the hall and Wesley led the way to a corner near the window of his large room. He directed Earl to a chair and Earl sat down. Then Wesley went to the cupboard to fetch another plate and more silverware.

He reapportioned the food and sat down. Earl placed his fingers lightly on the food and then he said, "Would you mind cutting the meat for me?" Welsey cut the meat into small pieces. He couldn't remember having watched a blind man eat before and he was fascinated. Earl's eyes were directed at Wesley's mouth and Wesley, embarrassed, turned his gaze to his own plate before he realized again that all the pictures that took shape behind Earl's eyes were of his own making, and for a moment Wesley looked at the blind man, trying to gather this fact into him, to accustom himself to its strangeness.

Earl stabbed a piece of the ham with his fork and raised it to his mouth. Wesley felt a shiver that started in the back of his head and ran down the length of his entire body. This disturbed him. After a moment Earl's plate was empty, but Wesley had eaten nothing. He had lost his appetite, the food seemed repulsive to him.

"Would you like some more, Earl?"

"Sure, if you've got plenty."

"Got more than I can eat." Wesley took Earl's plate away and replaced it with his own. Then he looked at the empty plate in his hand and something terrible happened: the plate sent a strangely soft shock into his hands that travelled through his body; this caused him to drop the plate and it smashed on the floor.

Earl stopped eating for a moment. He sat upright, cocked his head to one side; his large nostrils flared tensely as if they were instruments to hear through. But he said nothing and after a moment continued to eat.

Wesley brought out his broom and while he swept the broken pieces of dime-store pottery into the dustpan he wondered what had caused the dish to fall from his hand. Perhaps some electricity had been conducted from the battery of Earl's hearing aid; but this seemed improbable. He wondered if he might be squeamish about Earl's afflictions. If this were the case he must certainly teach himself to get over it.

After the meal the two men smoked several cigarettes while Earl, stimulated by questions from Wesley, told of the sickness, pneumonia, which had resulted in his loss of sight and impaired hearing. This had come about when he was seven years old. He told Wesley that his last visual memory was of snow falling on pine trees in the hills near his home in New Hampshire on the night his mother had driven him to the hospital. He spoke pleasantly and without bitterness for more than an hour and Wesley would have listened longer and willingly to this voice that came from a world so strange to him; but Earl rose to leave. He explained that the night was his best time for work. He carried into the streets a box of leather-goods made by the blind and sold them in restaurants and cafés, lunch counters and beer halls; he said that in the daytime, especially during this heat spell, few persons were willing even to stop and examine his wares.

He thanked Wesley for the meal and then he went out into the streets.

Now this small offering of a meal to an afflicted person is a usual and everyday occurrence in the world, but not in the world of Wesley Stuart. The fact that he lived in a city where there were other people should not be interpreted to mean that he lived with them or even among them; for in spite of appearances he had in him all the makings of a hermit and might as well have lived in the middle of the Mojave Desert.

Early in his life, in a small city in Central Ohio, Wesley had taken part in a war that was fought day and night in his own home; and in this war the weapons used had been of the most viciously subtle variety known to man: silence, withdrawal, a kind of passive hatred from which emanated death rays that worked more slowly but with a more terrible effectiveness than any imagined by the meanest of scientists: for the victim must go through his life on the surface unharmed, but inside of him, still mechanically pumping blood, lies a tiny poisoned corpse.

The issues at stake had been forgotten long before Wesley's birth; but as can happen in any war the fighting continued because neither side knew how to stop. Wesley at first had been more a witness than a target to all this quiet commotion and murder, but the circle of fire grew steadily larger until it included him. Harold and Irma Stuart, until their divorce—long after Wesley left home—had taken turns withdrawing: Harold Stuart would spend every second night drinking at a beer garden poker party; on alternate nights Irma Stuart would attend one of her clubs, chair a book discussion or play bridge. Wesley spent one evening with his father and the following with his mother: the first poring over school books and the second at play. For many years he worked at a puppet stage made from a large toilet-paper carton in which groceries had been delivered, but his father thought it was a doll's house of some sort and when Wesley began suddenly to grow taller, Harold Stuart's annoyance with this game reached its peak. He stuffed the puppets and the stage into an incinerator and lighted a match to them. That Saturday afternoon while this fire was still burning Wesley listened to a long and dispiteous lecture on the differences between childhood and maturity. His father had apparently given considerable drunken thought to the ways in which a "man" does not behave. He disapproved of each of the few friends Wesley had at one time and another managed to win; the truth was that he did not want them underfoot, they caused in him a peculiar disquiet which increased his unhappiness and so he discouraged or forbade these alliances. Wesley was left to continue in his solitude, but without the puppets; and when the time came he discovered the usual private amusement of which many fathers seem to know nothing.

But, undermined by a strong distrust of others, Wesley's imagination centred more and more in himself and there was a long period, perhaps two years or more, in which every word said to him had to be spoken twice. For it is known that a person's thoughts can travel no distance greater than the distance to the shelf; one may think of China, or the moon, and at the same time hear and see all that goes on about him, but when the thoughts are buried deep within the carnival mazes of his own heart, a person may as well be deaf and blind.

Between father and son then the situation was a simple one: they disliked one another with the quiet formality of estranged lovers. But Irma Stuart was another problem altogether. This was a woman whom Wesley alternately hated and loved. At times, early in his life, he had welcomed and even invited her affection, but just as often he had been repelled by it. She seemed boneless. Her face was yellow white. She had soft hysterical eyes. Her hands wiggled and crawled like white wrinkled worms. Except for the times when she laughed, which were too frequent, Irma Stuart smiled continually, but this apparently gay activity was more frightening to Wesley than a frown or a scream might have been. The desperation of a woman who screams is usually a temporary state, but the desperation of a woman who laughs in these haunting depthless tones is probably a permanent condition, a portrait of the soul. Even small children see these portraits and understand them. Each cackle from Irma Stuart's throat echoed an agony of unfulfilment, bitterness: the nerve show of a dead heart dressed in hysteria.

Often she seemed to pretend that Wesley did not exist, but these periods would be broken by sudden bursts of kindness, loving gestures, unexpected wisdoms. On one such occasion, when Wesley was seventeen, she signed a paper authorizing his enlistment in the Navy.

Wesley believed that with this separation he had won the long war against his father. But now and again in small ways that he understood and in ways too profound to be understood at all, it was clear that the war continued, that Wesley carried the enemy, his father, within himself. Certain words and ideas, tiny acts of destructiveness toward others, would bring about sudden flashes of clarity in which he could see in himself his father's image. At times even in the mirror the spectacle of that familiar brutality—eyes temporarily shrunken with hatred, mouth withdrawn to a mean bloodless slit—would suck the colour from his face and leave him white with dread. But a more dangerous similarity was his inability to cope with others. From any relationship not directly involved with earning his livelihood, he automatically withdrew. And he nurtured this isolation with the loving care of a mother for a child, for within it he was at peace.

This was something Wesley knew nothing of: this strange family of three which waged its endless war on the quiet battleground of his solitude: how like a mother he cooked and kept house and how like a father he thwarted the love that was in him and like an infant lay revelling in the false security of this twisted and solitary crib.

Wesley had learned carpentry in the Navy and now he worked building platforms and sets at a television station in Hollywood. But he did not want to live in that city. Some men might be attracted by the night-life that is supposed to go on in Hollywood but whenever Wesley remained there even until twilight a certain disquiet arose in him that would sometimes last for several days. Another carpenter named George Dunlap had once asked why Wesley lived in Pasadena. Wesley said he was not sure himself but it seemed to him everybody in Hollywood, even the people of the streets, were somehow hysterical, out of their minds. George said they'd never seemed that way to him and that ended it.

But Wesley had other reasons for preferring to drive back and forth each day. Some of these reasons he understood and others he did not think about. In the first place he liked to use his car. The weather in California is usually decent and you can drive with the top down and get sunshine on your face and arms except during the winter months but even they are mild and pass quickly. And in the second place he liked his apartment and did not want to give it up for new people, strangers, to live in. This room in the made-over attic of Mrs. Kromer's old frame house was only two blocks from the speedway connecting the two cities (he could drive it in twenty-seven minutes) and he had come to think of it as home.

His life was composed of these four major parts: himself, his apartment, his car and his bankbook. The job was not really a part of this. It merely relieved him of excess energies and allowed him to pay the rent on his apartment and the upkeep on his car and caused the figure in the bankbook to swell at a steady and reassuring rate. If he saved for anything at all, it was for insurance against change. Wesley failed to realize that all the money in the world could not purchase such a policy and the waste involved in hoping for it did not seem to offer any serious threat. He looked upon waste as somewhat less deteriorating than pain; and therefore he looked upon this lonely freedom from experience as a possession like his car, the apartment or his bankbook, a treasure to be cared for and protected.

2

One power a solitary person often holds over others is a certain inscrutable charm; there is about such a person an aura of other-worldly calm, a suggestion of mysteries unsolved, of depths unplumbed, some obscure promise of romance. And when this charm is coupled with youth, there is often a banging on his door by someone who, thinking it may be of value, has come to steal the secret.

Mrs. Faye Zelger Young lived on the first floor in a dark and untidy room across the hall from the landlady. She was a girl of medium height with small breasts and large hips and she called herself Miss Fay Zelger because for the past five years the Mrs. and the Young no longer applied and she could see no reason for using them: a Mrs. on a name tied a woman down. She had followed her husband to the West Coast in order to be with him during the weeks before he was sent overseas and then had stayed on here living on his allotment cheques. When the wire came announcing his death in the last days of the war, Faye was just eighteen. Her parents lived in a small town on the edge of a great swamp in the interior of Florida. Her daddy was away from home most of the time working for the government—inspecting trees, she thought, but she wasn't just sure—and her mamma was cranky. There was no reason to go back there, none that was worth the bus fare. Besides, after that terrible news Faye had been in the mood for a little sympathy and since her mother never had thought much of Sergeant Bernie K. Young—he had habits that made her nervous, made popping noises with chewing gum and scratched himself no matter who was around to see what it was that itched—it was not likely this cranky old woman, her own mother, would be much comfort to her.

The government sent an insurance cheque regularly but it was not large and Faye went to work selling cosmetics in a ten-cent store on Colorado Boulevard. Faye herself used nothing but lipstick and the customers bored her so that after three weeks she begged the manager to transfer her to some other counter—hardware, housewares, dry goods for men—anything but cosmetics would have fitted her just as perfectly as a glove. But he refused and she gave the job up, determined to skimp through as best she could on the government money. She moved into Mrs. Kromer's for six dollars a week and waited for something more suitable to come along.

Faye was pretty. She had light hair, naturally curly, and called herself a dark blonde. She was proud of this hair and aside from parting it on the left and trimming it with her own scissors, she let it do just as it pleased: fall in large soft waves down to her shoulders. Often it fell over her face, partly obscuring the vision of her right eye. If she were alone, Faye would screw up her mouth and blow the hair back where it belonged, but in the presence of someone who mattered to her she would do one of three things: roll her head to the right and jerk her head suddenly backward, lift her hand spread-fingered and deal with it directly, or simply let it fall and look at him out of one and a half eyes. Once at a cocktail bar in Hollywood she'd met a director who told her that if she'd cut her hair and work hard to get rid of that Southern accent, he'd see what he could do about getting her into pictures. She went to a beauty parlour on the Sunset Strip to have it cut by a man who was supposed to be famous for his work on picture people but he'd made an awful mess of it and she vowed once it grew out she'd never set foot in one of those places again. Once was enough. Then the director turned out to be a snake-in-the-grass and Faye wrote her mother that she'd had a good offer from the movies but the studio wanted her to change her personality and if they didn't like her the way she was, well, she was sorry, that's all, *damn* sorry.

Now when a person asked Faye what she did, she might tell him she was an actress. And if he asked what she'd done, she'd lift her shoulders and close her eyes and laugh: "What have I *not* done, my dear, what have I *not* done?" When pressed further on this subject or on any other for which the truth was inconvenient she would turn her face squarely to the person sitting next to her—perhaps it would be at a cocktail bar somewhere, some perfectly all-right place where *even a nun* could sit at the bar without anybody getting too smart for his pants—and smile, knitting her brows in a way that suggested some mysterious never-to-be-forgotten pain: "Lover," she would say, "if there is one subject that absolutely and surely depresses me, it is the past." And likely as not she would squeeze his hand, light a cigarette and ask him to tell her a story.

Wesley Stuart did not know Faye well at all. They had spoken often on the front porch and in the halls of the house and once at her suggestion she had come up to see his apartment. On this occasion they had smoked cigarettes together and talked quietly for a quarter of an hour and at the close of the visit she had extracted from Wesley the promise to invite her for dinner "some time soon", though it hadn't occurred to him that she might not only remember but hide in the halls waiting to arrange what would seem to be a chance encounter so that she might remind him of the promise and hold him to it.

On the morning following his evening with the blind man, Wesley found Faye once again waiting at the base of the stairwell. She had at first seemed to him a much older person, certainly as old as himself, for although her face was clear and fresh, the skin seemed to have lost that vaguely incandescent brightness of people still in their very early twenties. And her manner had seemed older: wise, and perhaps somewhat bored. He had admired the way her mouth attacked a cigarette while her eyes, hard and steady, remained focused on his, and her almost wicked quality of seeming incapable of surprise. But now, standing in the hallway with her hands behind her back and her tiny bosoms thrust forward, there was a nervous brightness in her eyes that made her seem almost coy, inexperienced. This made Wesley uncomfortable but he responded to her greeting with a smile and Faye walked with him down the hallway to the front door.

Mrs. Kromer was seated where he had left her the night before but she was no longer sucking a lemon. On her lap, unopened, was a large black book entitled *Morning Meditations* by Anna Hope Barneweller. Mrs. Kromer's hands were busy adjusting a large comb under the great untidy knot of greying brown hair that sat on top of her head. Mrs. Kromer, when the weather had been normal, was a talkative woman but these past few days she had lapsed into a silence that was only broken by incomplete phrases. She called these days a period for meditation.

Faye sat with her on the porch and the two women watched Wesley's car pull out from the curb. They followed it with their eyes until it turned into the speedway two blocks from the house.

"Drives too fast," said Mrs. Kromer. She worried about everyone she knew, but Mr. Stuart was one of the special burdens of her meditations. So were Faye and many of the other tenants. But Wesley Stuart in particular. Mrs. Kromer believed she could detect the needs, the fears, the inner tremblings of another entity as surely as a Geiger counter could detect the presence of radioactivity. Some persons, according to Anna Hope Barneweller, had this divine faculty and Mrs. Kromer believed she herself fitted the description in Mrs. Barneweller's book. Mrs. Barneweller also admonished these special persons, her readers, against unwise intervention in the affairs of others. Mrs. Kromer had constantly to restrain herself. But she believed privately that certain tiny seeds planted graciously from time to time might find some degree of fertility in their minds.

She believed she had come to understand the source of Mr. Stuart's problem and that she knew the exact nature of the peril to which his soul was exposed. Certain deductions she had made simply from observation: his eyes, for example, told of worry and sleepless nights. They were china blue and as bright as new lacquer but the whites were flecked with red and just below the eyes she had noticed the subtle beginnings of death, a process which, though it might continue for another fifty years, was nevertheless in evidence on the vaguely dark and discoloured sacs of skin; this indicated a troubled soul. His nose dipped upward, little-boy-fashion she called it, and his mouth, because the nose was small, seemed extravagantly large; the skin of his lips was thin and it windowed the dark colour of blood underneath, profoundly red, the lips of a man in fever. His head was of a size reasonably proportionate to his slight body, and his hair was curly and blond, almost white. A pate of pink showed through at the back of his head and the hairline had begun definitely to recede.

During the years in which Mr. Stuart had occupied the room on the fourth floor, Mrs. Kromer had gathered only the most ordinary factual data on his private affairs: he paid his rent regularly, he did not drink whisky though he kept a bottle of it in a bureau drawer, he smoked but she was quite certain he did not smoke in bed, his sole correspondent was his mother in Ohio, he made heaps of money somewhere in Hollywood, and he was a lone wolf sort of person who did not entertain often.

Aside from these facts she had another more important piece of information gathered some weeks ago in the middle of a rainy night. On a tour of the building to check and close all doors and windows against the storm, she had passed through the hall outside Mr. Stuart's room at two in the morning just in time to hear certain strange and irregular sounds from within. His voice was calling out in the night. He seemed to be strangling. She listened for a moment to the choked cries intermingled with a forlorn kind of weeping. Fearless, protected as always by her belief in a world of predominant good, she had knocked on the door. The sounds continued. She quickly singled out the master key from the large ring hanging at her waist, unlocked the door, entered and turned on the light.

Mr. Stuart had sat up in bed. His angry eyes glossy as one gone mad, he stared at her and shouted some unrepeatable curse. Mrs. Kromer walked directly to his bed, raised her arm, paused for a moment to eye her target: within a fragment of a second, her hand had landed with a great smacking sound on his face.

He began to cry.

Mrs. Kromer went to the sink under the window in his kitchen alcove. She soaked a dish towel in cold water from the tap and, returning to his side, begged him to lie down. He obeyed instantly and Mrs. Kromer applied the wet towel to his face and informed him he had been dreaming. Wesley began feebly to protest that it was not a dream, someone had actually been trying to... *Trying to what?* Shocked into more complete wakefulness by contact with the cold towel, he could no longer remember the details of the dream.

Mrs. Kromer returned to the kitchen area and lighted a fire under a pan of water. This was for tea. Then she drew a chair to the edge of his bed and sat down.

"Someone trying to do what?" she said.

To please her, Wesley invented an answer: "Trying to climb in that window."

The time had come, thought Mrs. Kromer, to plant a small seed. She pointed at the window next to his bed. "That one? Four storeys up? Mr. Stuart, the only person *tall* enough to climb in that window is God. And when He comes in you got nothing to worry about."

She told him some more about God and though Wesley did not listen carefully, he liked the sound of her voice. There was strength in her big ugly barefootedness and her lantern jaw swung with such homely vigour when she spoke that he could not for a moment doubt the goodness of her intentions. When she had brewed the tea and poured it into cups, Mrs. Kromer began to inquire about the general nature of his dreams and while they drank the tea Wesley told of an incident he had dreamed several times:

He is called down to the morgue to identify a person killed on a sidewalk by an automobile that has gone wild. Wesley is led into a large room with shiny black walls. In the centre of this room is a body reclining on a slab of white marble. An attendant uncovers the body and Wesley begins to weep; in the dream he sees himself standing over the slab weeping aloud like a child. A friend appears and conducts Wesley from the room into a vestibule that is filled with people who watch him weep and, unashamed, shouting hysterically, the waters of his sorrow rivering down over his red face, he is helped into a waiting taxi. When Wesley awakens from this dream his face is usually wet with real tears and for several minutes his mind, in an effort to identify the face of the corpse, stares at the memory of the dreamed-up slab. No face appears there however and this is a painful frustration, this struggle in vain to discover whose dream death has caused him to weep.

"I see," said Mrs. Kromer sadly, sympathetically, her eyes focused on the sloping wall over his head. "Mm-*hmmm!* Now I understand many things about you I'd given plenty of wonder to. Why it is you're a bachelor for instance is all perfickly clear to me now." She lowered her voice and looked into his eyes. "You know who it was you seen on that slab, Mr. Stuart?"

Wesley shook his head. Mrs. Kromer took a long swallow of tea and sank back into her chair. "It was y'self!"

Wesley was annoyed that she should seem so confident her interpretation was the correct one; but he wanted to hear more. "Does that mean I'm going to die in a car accident?"

"Not a thing of the kind. Forget that, son. All you got to do is remember this: the only death a living person ever mourns is his own."

Wesley tried to hide his irritation behind a smile. "But I'm not *dead.*"

Mrs. Kromer's mouth opened in a sympathetic grin that showed false teeth and dark red artificial gums. She smiled for a long time and then she said. "Are you sure about that, Mr. Stuart?"

After a moment, she rose. "Maybe you'd like to get some sleep." But before she reached the door, Wesley's voice had stopped her. "Mrs. Kromer!"

"Yes, son?"

"I thought you might like more tea."

"Well," she said. "I surely would."

And soon she was embarked on a discussion of a certain theory she believed in: namely, that when a man gives up his belief in love, his soul dies. Everyone has some certain person cut out for him by the Almighty and if a man doesn't ever happen to have the privilege of meeting his certain person, he must not brood on this sad destiny. The Bible said self-pity stunk and so the only thing left to do was to devote the balance of his lonely sojourn, just as she had done, to doing good for others— and certainly each tiny act of benevolence would be returned to him a thousand-fold. *At least!*

"Now," she concluded, placing her cool hand over his hot moist one, "you must thank God for sending me up here to interpret your dream for you."

Wesley could not resist asking if he should also thank God for murdering his soul but the moment the words were out, he regretted them. Mrs. Kromer removed her hand from his and as it returned to her lap the forefinger waved to and fro warningly; "Woe betide him who mocketh my words," she said, inventing a quotation. Then her great jaw swung back and forth once again and she continued, "You see, Mr. Stuart, you and me just might— just *might*, I say, be bearing the same cross."

"You mean you've never met your certain person either?"

"Never *met* him exactly—but I know who he is. My certain person lives in China. Comes to me quite often in my meditations. But Lord, I'm an old woman, Mr. Stuart. It's too late. They's four hundred million people in China. I looked it up once."

Wesley tried to imagine Mrs. Kromer in the Orient, her great fleshless bones, her large occidental eyes, hyperthyroid and slightly wild, her long feet bound in delicate silk sandals, seated cross-legged under an Asiatic sun, a parasol over her head...

"It was never intended. Not for *this* lifetime. But I'm a patient woman. What was intended was I should make a mistake, so I did. That was Bartholomew. After a few years he wandered away, but I don't blame him. 'F he hadn't, *I* would've. Providence moveth in mysterious ways."

Wesley was grateful to the old hag for her kindness; her presence had been diverting and he was comforted. He smiled and Mrs. Kromer, who felt that this smile alone had rewarded her, told him so.

They fell silent and for a long time there was only the pleasant noise of tea being drunk in the night, the swallowing, the stirring, the intimate clink of cups on saucers. When he looked at Mrs. Kromer her great eyes were half closed but in the centres of the pupils he saw a strong and tiny light shining as motionlessly as a star. She spoke and her voice was small.

"I think about that man a whole lot."

"Who?"

"That Chinaman," she said.

3

Faye Zelger spent most of her Wednesday morning on the front porch looking through back issues of *Life* and *Look*. Along about noon she wandered up to Colorado Boulevard and ate her lunch in a drugstore. There were big fans grinding the air into motion, false icicles gleamed on the pie cases; and with this illusion of coolness she was able to collect her thoughts.

She wanted to make a special impression on Wesley Stuart when she appeared for dinner on the fourth floor at seven-thirty. Faye wasn't sure she *liked* him or anything like that but he seemed always so far off into himself that it might be fun to pull him out a little bit, not to tease him exactly but maybe to make him nervous, show him somebody else was alive besides himself. She didn't want to start anything but it just *got* her the way he didn't mind the hot weather and the smog and smiled at poor Mrs. Kromer squeezing lemons all over herself to keep cool, and ran up the stairs two at a time as if there was something just *marvellous* up there waiting for him, and in the mornings the way his car zoomed forward even before he had the door shut: close your eyes and count five, Alacazam! he's half-way to Hollywood.

Smart!

She hoped he realized there was at least one party wasn't impressed with his working in Hollywood; principally Miss Faye Zelger of Oskachee, Florida. Besides he was in television which was *not* movies and if he'd ever seen half as many stars as she had, Wesley'd probably fall flat on his face. Faye was laughing inside and when she saw herself in the mirror behind the pie case, there was a smile on her face. She had a good long afternoon to plan her entrance and Honey, she told herself, *you*'ll make him wiggle if you have to walk in naked, stark raving naked.

Faye gulped down the last of her ice water and hurried out of there but the manager or somebody who acted like he *thought* he was the manager shouted after her to come back and pay her check. Embarrassing? The people on the sidewalk stared at her like she was Tokyo Rose or somebody just as godawful. Probably tourists, she thought. She went back to the cashier and paid her bill. The manager tried to smile at her but she cut him dead and told the cashier to kindly tell Mr. Priss it'd be a merry Christmas in April before he saw *her* again and maybe if the food was half-ways decent the customers wouldn't forget to pay for it. Of course the cashier wouldn't condescend to answer, his black bow tie probably choked the voice right out of his skinny little throat. And if the tie didn't, she'd like to have a try at it herself. Black bow tie in this weather? What'd he think his tacky little drugstore was, the Mocombo night club? Lord how she hated prissy men!

The smog caused her eyes to itch but Faye knew better than to rub. That starts them burning and they turn red and stay red for days. She hurried home and by the time she reached the front porch her dress was soaked with perspiration. Mrs. Kromer stood behind the screen door swatting flies.

"You look flustered, Missie."

"I expect I do," Faye said.

"Somethin' wrong?"

"Oh nothin' atall, I was just flatly accused of bein' a thief is all—by some fairy in a drugstore no less. Humiliated before the entire city of Pasadena for fifty-nine cents plus tax." Faye opened the door. "Got half a notion to sue," she said and started down the hall.

"Shame on you," said Mrs. Kromer.

Faye stood still. "Shame on *which?*"

"Not very sweet, those words you use, milady."

"What words?"

"What you said that man was."

Faye shrugged and smiled. "Huh! It's a known fact they can't stand a pretty girl." She continued down the hall.

By five-thirty, after a long sleepless rest and lukewarm bath, Faye had devised her plan: dolling up surely would be a fat mistake. She would walk in looking like hell itself, perhaps in overalls, breathless, hair all a mess, no lipstick; and late, twenty minutes at least—or just long enough for Wesley Stuart to get it into his blue-eyed head that at least one person didn't give the tiniest damn. But at six-thirty she had decided on lipstick and just as she was about to walk out the door, Faye caught a glimpse of herself in a mirror: her hair looked like Spanish moss and it wouldn't do. So she brushed it. At a quarter of seven, radiant in a sleeveless summer cotton dress—simple lines, pale yellow—Faye knocked on Wesley's door. "Yoo-hoo," she sang.

Wesley was tearing a head of lettuce apart with his fingers. He smiled a bright smile. "Hi. Make yourself at home." Faye sat down and Wesley said, "You look very nice. Like a million dollars."

"Thank you, Wesley, though I don't know why I should, I've had a perfectly miserable day."

"Oh? I'm sorry to hear it."

Faye expected him to question her about the crisis implied in her remark; she waited, and then Wesley said, "I'm a little slow tonight. Haven't even got the table set."

Faye sprang to her feet. "Do let me help, Wesley."

"Oh no. No." He was emphatic.

Faye eyed a package of cigarettes on the stand next to her.

"May I smoke one of your cigarettes then?"

"Of course. Help yourself."

"I love king-size. Is this that new brand you can smoke underwater?"

Wesley took three yellow plates and three yellow saucers from the cupboard and set them on the table. "What'd you say?"

"Oh, I was just makin' conversation. Do I see *three?*"

"Three what?"

"Places. Are you settin' *three* places?"

"Oh yeah, yeah. I meant to—uh..."

"You meant to tell me. Well, I won't pretend I'm not disappointed. Who is this third party? Some glamorous Hollywood creature?"

"It's the man across the hall. He stopped in to say hello, and I thought all this food—I bought too much anyway."

Faye was furious but it wouldn't do to show it. She sucked quietly at her cigarette and after a moment she said, "Wesley, I don't want you to hate me or think anything dreadful but I just—I don't really think I could face it after the day I've had."

"Face what?"

"That man. I know it's awful but he makes me feel—I don't know *how* he makes me feel but "

"You mean because he's blind?"

"I suppose so. And deaf. That's terrible, isn't it?"

"No, it's not terrible. I felt funny about it at first. Last night "

"He ate here *last* night? And he's eatin' here tonight, too?"

"Faye, I don't think he's got much money. He sells leather billfolds."

"Yes, I know. In beer gardens."

"And his mother sends him a little each week. She works in a mill somewhere in New England. I guess I felt sorry for him."

"You mean, Wesley, he told you all those personal things, just like that, to a stranger?"

"Why shouldn't he?"

"Well, he's probably just as sweet as he can be but don't you think it's funny? Hasn't he got an awful nerve?"

"I don't think so. Blind people are probably—you know, lonesome. And he can't hardly hear either, don't forget that."

Faye smoked quietly for a moment and watched Wesley who stood at the table cutting large slices from a cheesecake. He seemed so contented that Faye wanted to walk over to the table and pick up a piece of the cheesecake with her bare hands and grind it into his face. Instead she ground out her cigarette and walked over to stand opposite him.

She rested her elbows on the table and held her face in her hands. "Wesley?" she began, "what would you think of Faye if she asked you for a rain check. 'Cause honey, I can relax with you alone I'm sure, but strangers always make me fidget and I'm so nervous to start with this evenin' I'd probably make *mis*erable company. You can understand that, can't you?"

"I'll be disappointed," he said, "but I wouldn't want you to be—well, uncomfortable."

"I had a hunch you'd be sweet about it."

Earl appeared at the door. He said hello and Wesley shouted to him to come in and sit down. Earl wore a blue sport shirt open at the throat and he was cleanly shaven; his face shone, he smelled of shaving lotion and his dark hair was slicked back with water. Faye watched as Wesley conducted him to a chair and then she lighted another cigarette and moved to Earl's side. "Remember me, honey?" she said. "I met you on the front porch yesterday."

Earl lifted his head and adjusted the volume on his hearing aid.

Wesley shouted to him from the table: "You remember Faye Zelger, the girl who lives downstairs?"

Earl smiled. "Is she here?"

Faye, flattered by the smile, rested her hand on his forearm.

"Right here, Earlzie," she shouted. "How's business? Sellin' lots of belts and billfolds and things?"

"Not too many," he said. "You going to be here for dinner?"

"If Wesley'll let me. Wesley? Can I stay for dinner?"

Wesley let her know she was welcome to do just as she pleased.

"You talking to me?" Earl said.

Faye leaned over and spoke directly into the microphone on Earl's chest. "Why don't you turn the volume up, honey? Then a girl won't have to shout so." She touched the microphone with her hand. "Here, let me show you."

"Can't turn it any louder," Earl said.

"Course you can." She twisted the tiny button on the side of the instrument and then, quietly, she said, "Now Earlzie, how's business?"

Earl frowned and gripped the chair arms with his hands.

"I said it was none too good."

"There! You heard every word I said."

Wesley watched with interest and then he said, "You shouldn't do that, Faye. Maybe it's hard on the battery."

"That's foolish. He can get another one. A person ought to use what they got while they got it. Isn't that right, Earlzie?"

Earl adjusted the volume to its proper level. "Not always, Faye. It hurts my ear, gives me a headache."

Faye hid her face in her hands and gasped with remorse. Then she whispered to Wesley: "I'm sorry, Wesley, I just don't know how to act with him. Don't you think I better come back sometime when it's just the two of us?"

"Whatever you say. Only I don't think you should whisper."

"Well, I'm *sorry.*" Faye made a miserable little attempt at laughter. "I'm not usually so awful, it's just this dreadful day I've had." Then returning to Earl, she shouted, "I'll be seein' you, Earl, I'm on the front porch quite a bit." She squeezed his hand. "G'bye."

Faye ran down the three flights of stairs and down the hall to the front porch. But the chairs were empty and she did not want to sit alone. A fat old woman walked slowly past the house pushing a baby carriage and on the steps of the house across the street a red glare from a cigarette moved lazily to someone's lips. But it was dark and she could not see who the person was.

4

Three weeks passed but the weather did not change. On certain nights a coolness set in and one could sleep with less discomfort but the smog thickened and every day the sun shone with a muted grey light that was not sunshine at all but a silvery and grimy glare like the light of hell itself; you would think some devil had taken all the oxygen from the air and replaced it with steel filings and itching powder.

Now Earl Walker sat across the table from Wesley Stuart each morning and each night. At breakfast there was not much conversation. Wesley would explain before he left the house just what was in the cupboards and in the refrigerator and at lunch-time Earl could help himself. By this time Earl had not only learned to find what he wanted but had caused certain changes to be made in the furniture arrangements of Wesley's apartment: the dining-table had been pulled out from the wall because Earl had bumped his head getting in and out; and now the radio was in a different place, next to a comfortable chair where Earl could sit and listen without adjusting the volume of his hearing aid. Under the chair he kept his bedroom slippers and to the right of the chair was a smoking stand he could flick ashes into without moving his arm more than a couple of inches. He had offered to do the dish-washing while Wesley was at work but even though he promised to use soap and get the dishes as clean as anyone could, Wesley told him to leave them; there was no need for Earl to spend so long doing what he himself could do quickly and effortlessly in the evenings.

Wesley did not feel imposed upon for Earl was the kind of companion he liked, one who never began a conversation but who seemed always to be willing to speak when he was spoken to on any subject whatever, even himself, and Wesley could end a discussion at any moment he chose simply by remaining silent. When he wanted to be alone he had only to hint at this and Earl would return to his own room or start out on his round of the cafés and beer halls; or, since he, Wesley, was unseen and only imperfectly heard, he felt he could be alone even in Earl's presence.

It was as if Wesley had continued to inhabit the fourth floor by himself but with a totally new kind of solitude. At first there had been inconveniences, the subtle changes that creep into an apartment and a life when a new person enters, but now he had become accustomed to carrying a heavier load of groceries up the stairs and a larger bag of garbage down to the street. Whatever had caused his loss of appetite during that first meal seemed now to have increased it. For there was some contagion in the obvious pleasure Earl took in his food. Once Wesley had remarked about this and Earl told him that when he drank milk he pictured in his mind the cow eating wild flowers, when he ate an apple he saw the tree in blossom and when he tasted something sweet he saw black men loading sugar-cane on to a great white ship; and these pictures added flavours to the food that otherwise would not exist.

Now Wesley was more anxious than ever to spend his evenings quietly in his own home and in the late afternoon he drove faster across the speedway, ran more quickly than ever up the stairs to the fourth floor and prepared elaborate substantial meals in place of the quick carry-out salads and cold cuts from the delicatessen which had previously satisfied him.

One evening after dinner Earl withdrew from his pocket an envelope that contained a letter from his mother. He placed it on the table and as Wesley poured the coffee, Earl said, "Would you read this to me?" Wesley suspected from his tone that Earl anticipated something disagreeable in the letter. Then Earl said, "My mother always says I should get a minister to read her letters to me." He laughed in a particularly mirthless way which Wesley had learned to interpret; it meant something was troubling him. "But I don't know any ministers," he added.

Wesley slit the envelope with a breadknife and Earl nervously lighted a cigarette. He sat forward in his chair, frowning as he listened:

"Dear Earl my son—

"Your letter was slow reaching here. You have to put air mail on the envelope or else a air mail stamp or else it travels regular by train. Too bad you have heat as it is nice here. I don't like to ball you out but that lady wrote me again that she would make trouble for you for not paying up. She said 95 was how much you owe but she would settle if I send 50 in little bits at a time."

Wesley thought this mention of personal finances might embarrass Earl. He stopped reading and tried to laugh as he said, "Maybe you *better* get a preacher to read this."

"What?"

"I said this is getting a little personal. You want me to go on with it?"

"Yes, please."

The handwriting had a pinched quality as if it had been written only with great effort by stiff fingers. The letter itself made him think of nudity, as if her tortured hand and badly spelled words were some indecent show of wounded flesh in a vaguely private zone. He continued to read:

"Son you make it hard and I know it is not easy but people take care of themselves can not take care of you. You think so and end up oweing. I work part time and the 15 will have to go to her this week or she will make trouble as she promises. The mill has bad business now but may pick up in fall the supervisor says. You live where you want but there are worst things than cold weather so maybe you will come here. But if I send again I will send the ticket and not $. I don't like to scold but you do things you have no right to and I am your mother. Well keep cool, son. Why don't you go to a minister to read your mail to you? That is proper not a stranger. Well keep cool son.

love your Mother"

Earl was silent for a moment and then he stood up and said, "That woman's crazy."

"Who, your mother?"

"No, my old landlady. I told her I'd pay when I could, but she kept my typewriter when I moved. Now she's got my mother all worked up."

Wesley showed him the place where his typewriter was kept, on the floor of his closet. He told Earl he could use it whenever he liked. Earl twisted the letter between his fingers and then he began to tear small pieces from it. Finally, he placed the letter in his pocket and, without a word, picked up his walking stick and left the room. A few minutes later Wesley saw Earl pass his doorway. He was still frowning and the cardboard box of leather goods was tucked under his arm.

When Wesley had washed the dishes and put his apartment in order, he sat on the edge of the bed. Later, when he looked at the clock, he realized that thirty minutes had passed and he could not remember what he had been thinking; but he had memorized every irregularity in the pale green wall of his sleeping alcove and the muscles in his thighs tensed and untensed every time the clock went tick-tock. Then, searching about for something to occupy him, he stood up and wandered about the room.

He heard footsteps, light and quick, on the stairway and since they could not be Earl's, he went to the door. It was Faye. Even though she was smiling brightly and spoke with a singer's tones, she seemed unhappy.

"I was settin' on the veranda when Earl passed by. He said you were up here all by yourself and I took a chance you might want some company. D'you mind?"

Wesley wasn't certain whether he wanted company or not. There had been a time, before the summer, when he would have given Faye some quick answer: that he was busy or tired or on his way out. But he had lost some of his former contentedness with solitude.

"Not at all," he said. "I have to write some letters before I go to bed though, but..."

"Oh, Wesley, just *say* so. I thought ____"

"No, come on in. I've got time for a cigarette at least."

Faye smiled and walked past him. "It's *so* pleasant up here, Wesley, truly pleasant. I don't know why, bein' next t' the roof, but I just love it. Always have since that first day."

Wesley sat in Earl's chair next to the radio. Faye stood smiling at him for a moment, solicitously, and this made him uneasy. But not knowing what else to do he returned her smile. Finally, Faye said, "Honey, you look wearyish. Why don't you stay right there comfortable and let Faye fix you some iced tea. In a tall glass."

"I haven't got any tall glasses, but there's tea in the refrigerator. On the top shelf in a milk bottle."

"Oh goody, shall we have some?" She chattered as she removed ice cubes from a tray and poured the tea. "I've been so *restless* all day! This whole summer I've been actin' like a crazy woman. It's not like me either, I'm usually just as calm! O'course, you don't know me, not really, Wesley, but I am. Usually that is. But with this weather—well, you'd think I was possessed by a whole tribe of devils of some Saint Vitus, I can't sit still. What d'you suppose it is, maybe?"

Wesley only half listened. "Maybe the weather."

"Weather? Why most people it perfectly paralyses. Except you of course. Wesley, I do envy you, always have. *Nothin'* seems to bother you, simply nothin'! I do admire that so in a man. Far as you're concerned we could all just drop dead, an' it wouldn't bother you an iota. I don't mean you're not *hu*man, but just sort of above it all. Did I offend you?"

"Oh no. You didn't offend me."

" 'Cause I meant it as a compliment. It's part of bein' intelligent, I think. A person like you a girl could prob'ly tell anything at all to and you wouldn't even bat an eye. I like that in a man, just to be a person's self with him. Sugar?"

"Huh?"

"You want sugar?" She laughed. "You thought I was callin' you sweet names, didn't you?"

"Yes please. One heaping."

"I talk too much, don't I? Go on, admit it. I do!"

She handed him the glass of tea and then she drew a chair from the kitchen table and sat facing him.

Wesley said, "I'd always rather listen than talk."

"That's what so many people say. They say I may talk too much but I do it so amusingly they don't mind to sit and listen. *I* don't think I'm amusing though. It's just this summer nervousness. Oh how this dress *clings* to me. Weather like this I'd as soon be a dragonfly in the swamp somewhere. *They* keep cool. You ever been to Flahrida?"

"Nope, never. What's it like?"

"You know what it's like as well as I do. You see *The Yearling?* That picture with Jane Wyman? *Who*, by the way, I don't care atall for!"

"I'm not sure."

"She is the drabbest thing!—But Flahrida's just like that, beauty everywhere. O'course the people're diff'rent. The movies make 'em like a bunch of hillbillies. But they're really more like me nowadays. Just—ordinary."

Oh, thought Wesley, but *you're* not ordinary. But he could not bring himself to say it.

"I'm so glad I had the nerve to come up here, Wesley. I was afraid you were mad at me the way I acted about Earl. This tea's s'good and it's the first time I've been comfy the whole day. Except—Wesley, I don't think I can stand this dress another minute. What if I' just slip it off and set here in m'slip?"

Wesley was not certain he had heard correctly. "You want to take your *dress* off?"

"M'petticoat covers everything important. We're both intelligent, aren't we?"

"What if—what if Earl should come up here? Or Mrs. Kromer? How would that look?"

"Mrs. Kromer wouldn't come up here!" She leaned forward and smiled. "What about Earl, honey? He's *blind!* Remember, like a bat!"

"Well, go ahead. If you'll be more comfortable."

"Thank Gawd!" Faye stood up and took hold of her dress by the skirt and pulled it over her head. Suddenly there was an emergency. *"Help!* I'm smotherin'! Wesley!"

Wesley stood up. "What d'you want *me* to do?"

"Help me, honey, please. M'head's caught."

Wesley unfastened the hook at the back of her neck and helped pull the dress over her head. Faye looked at him sheepishly with a false frown. "Claustrophobia," she said. "I'm always afraid I'll smother m'self t'death."

Wesley's embarrassment sent blood to his face. He went to the refrigerator to refill his glass. "Some more tea?" he said.

"No thanks, but I feel a thousand per cent better."

When they were seated once more, Faye said, "With some men I might feel naked like this, but with you not at all." Then she turned her eyes from him. "I guess I do like you pretty much, Wesley. I feel silly saying so, but..."

"But with me you feel you can," he said; the irony with which he had tried to colour his voice did not affect her one whit. Wesley began to wonder how soon he could get her clothed and out the door. She leaned forward and placed her hand on his.

"I know men, Wes, and I can tell a kind one when he comes along. How many I ask you would let a person barge right in on their privacy like this? Not very damn many, honey, excuse my French but it's true."

"Oh, I don't know about that, Faye."

"Nope, nope, you're wrong! A single girl, even though she may be a widow, learns an awful lot about life. O'course you did know I was a widow."

"Yes, I guess I did."

"Well it's not very easy, honey. Now let's talk about you."

He smiled. "I'm *not* a widow."

Faye laughed: "Of course you're not." Then she moved quickly to his side and mussed his hair with her fingers.

"Oh, you *are* fun, dammit all." And then she dropped her hand to his chin and drew his face to her breast. "Sweet, too."

Wesley took hold of her wrist firmly and pulled her hand from his face. With her arm still in his grip, he stood and faced her.

Faye said, "You *hurt* me! Whatever's wrong anyhow? Heavens, I was only foolin' around. Aren't we both intelligent?"

He released her arm and Faye held her hurt wrist tenderly in her free hand. Then, raising it to her face, she caressed it with her lips. As she looked up at Wesley, her brows knitted in mock pain, she said, "Goddam you, honey, you're *strong*"

"I sure didn't mean to hurt you, Faye."

"Oh, was that supposed to feel good?"

"Why don't you put on your dress and we'll go sit on the front porch. Finish our cigarettes, drink our tea."

Faye smiled at him. "If that's what you want more than anything else in the world—then that's just what we'll do. 'Cept I'm not putting on this dress, not for all o' Carter's little pills."

When they had reached the landing on the second floor, Fay turned to Wesley and held his arm for a moment. "I suppose it did seem to you I was actin' like a—you know, just dreadful, like some floozie. But I hope you know it's not ____ "

Wesley interrupted, "You mean you just felt that with me you could!"

Faye turned angrily and hurried down the hall. Wesley followed close behind, laughing gently. "Hey, you're not sore, are you? I was just trying to be funny."

Faye did not look at him when she answered. "You make a girl feel like about thirty cents. Honestly!"

Mrs. Kromer was asleep on the front porch but the slam of the screen door awakened her.

"Oh!" Faye said, "I thought you'd be in bed. We were just goin' to sit for a minute or two. You know, cool off, as if that was possible, Lord."

Mrs. Kromer eyed Faye curiously; her mouth fell open and her big jaw rested on her chest. "What's goin' on? What happened to you?"

"Nothin', why?" Faye said. Mrs. Kromer sat forward.

"W-w-where's your—your dress?"

"Oh, I was just up at Wesley's and it got so hot we'd like to screamed. So I took off m'dress."

Mrs. Kromer stared stupidly at Wesley. There was no judgment in her tone, only profound curiosity. "Just the two of you up there?" Wesley was not certain what she was thinking but the struck dumb look on her face amused him.

"Don't worry about it, Mrs. Kromer. Faye's safe with me,"

Faye looked into his face for a moment, her eyes opened wide, and she said loudly: "Safe! Did you say *safe?*" And then she began to laugh. Wesley felt the blood rush to his face again as her laughter rose. Faye threw herself into the chair next to Mrs. Kromer. She turned to her and said, "Honey, did you hear what I heard?"

Mrs. Kromer was puzzled. "I think I did. Why?"

"Oh nothin', but it just struck me. Sit down, Wes."

But Wesley remained standing, his toes gripped firmly at the soles of his shoes as if he sought to plant himself more securely to the wooden planks of the porch floor. He looked at Faye and he saw her eyes glittering wildly into his face and now Mrs. Kromer was staring at him too.

"A girl couldn't be *safer*" Faye said. "She just couldn't!"

She began to laugh once more but this time there was hysteria in her tones. Wesley wanted to take hold of her throat and choke the voice from it but he stood there and listened while the whole world and even the darkness itself seemed to crack open and crumble under the hammering blows of these nightmare sounds.

5

There is an all-night coffee place on the corner of Green and Marengo across the street from the Queen City Bus Depot. It is a small white building set alone on the edge of a parking lot. Among the persons who stop here are bus and taxi drivers, workers on their way home from the swing shift at the aircraft factories, and people waiting for the bus to Hollywood.

When Earl Walker opened the door at midnight, the counterman shouted, "Hi pal! Sit down."

Earl smiled at the counterman and to the place itself. "Is that you, Stokes?"

"Yeah, it's me." Stokes's voice was deep and harsh. He was in his middle thirties and black hair grew thick on his chest and arms.

"Where'll I sit?" Earl said.

"Anywhere. The place is empty." Stokes came out from behind the counter and conducted Earl to the stool nearest the door. "The fan's broke down, but you might get a breeze here."

Earl placed his cardboard box on the counter and hung his cane on the edge of it. After a moment he heard a dish touch the counter in front of him.

Stokes said, "Cream and sugar, right? And a glazed dough-nut. Have I got a memory?"

Earl would have preferred milk but the coffee had been poured and he knew Stokes was sensitive.

"Doin' yourself any good, Earl?"

"I got some prospects. Did a fella named John ask for me tonight?"

"John? Nope, no Johns, pal."

Earl sipped the coffee but it was steaming hot and so he smoked and waited for it to cool. Some time later, after several customers had arrived, eaten and left again, he said, as if no time had elapsed at all: "Because I'm lookin' for him."

"What you say, Earl?"

"He's supposed to meet me here at midnight."

"Who's that, Earl? Who you talking about?"

"Fella named John." He extended his arm to Stokes.

"My watch right, Stokes?"

"Yeah. Ten after one. Say, Earl, how come you wear a watch? I mean..."

Earl smiled. "No crystal on it and the numbers stick up. Braille."

"You know that's goddam clever," said Stokes. Then he waited on a lady who had come in, a nurse who wanted strong coffee to take out. When she had left, others came in and Stokes was busy for a while and then there was loud noise in the parking lot and six young boys, hot-rod drivers, came in for hamburgers and when they had left, Stokes said, "Earl, I don't think this John's gonna show. It's two-thirty. You got some important business with him?"

"Important to me," Earl said. "He took a billfold last night, said he was going to show his brother-in-law and bring it back tonight. Either that or pay me the six-fifty."

"Where'd you meet this creep?"

"In a bar on Fair Oaks Avenue."

"Fair Oaks! What, some dive? And you never seen him before?"

"No, but I talked to him quite a bit."

"Well, buddy," Stokes said, "I think you been had."

Earl was silent for a moment. Then he said. "You don't mind me waiting here, do you, Stokes?"

"*Hell* no! Want some more coffee?"

Earl sat in this coffee place until morning but the man named John did not appear. At six-thirty, Earl stood and withdrew a change purse from his pocket. "Stokes?"

"Yeah?"

"How much?"

"Nothin'. You kept me company."

"I *want* to pay for it," Earl said.

"Naw, forget it."

"I don't want to forget it," he said firmly. Then, after a moment, he added quietly: "Why don't you let me owe you?"

"Why owe me?" Stokes said. "I'll never remember anyway. I got a memory like a pig. I can't even remember when I was born. Nineteen-nineteen, I think."

Earl spoke softly, "Anybody else here but us?"

"The place is empty. Why?"

"Look, Stokes," Earl said, "I'd rather owe you 'cause then when I come back again you won't think I'm a bum."

Stokes looked at Earl for a long time. Then, quietly, he said, "Okay, pal; you owe me."

Earl picked up his cardboard box and his cane and started for the door. Stokes reached it first and opened it. He took Earl's arm and said, "Buddy, listen a minute, will you? You shouldn't go around trusting people. Not these days." To emphasize the point he was about to make, he lifted his hand, and failing to realize the gesture would be lost on Earl, he pointed toward the ceiling with his middle finger. "They'll screw you every time."

Earl was silent for a long time and then he grinned. "Stokes, I just clipped you for seventy-five cents, didn't I?"

"*Me?* Hell no. You said you'd *owe* me!"

Earl started out the door. "That's right. And John owes me. So long, Stokes."

For a long time, perhaps a year or more, Wesley Stuart had, before going to bed each night, covered his mirror by draping a towel over the door of his medicine chest. There was a reason for this: if he came to it newly awakened, faced it unprepared, his mirror held within it the power to spoil an entire day: some terrifying emptiness in the set of his mouth, a certain dark and hawklike hunger in his eyes, a total portrait of misery so profound that it at times caused him to weep, confronted him with such fascinating horror that he could seldom look away until it had damaged his spirit and left him weak with depression. Though he never thought of it in this way, it was the face of one who seemed destined to become a mystic but who had not yet found his god or his cult, in whom there was only the need and the hunger, the void itself, a great windowless temple inside where, while the body slept, demons flitted and played, sucking at the spirit. The alarm clock, the radio, breakfast, all of these were a part of the imperfect daily exorcism; but perhaps a more important part of this process had been Wesley's facility for repressing his memory of them when they persisted.

But at some time during this summer of heat and smog he had given up this practice of covering the mirror at night, for he found no further need to prepare in this way his daytime attitude. Now in the mornings when the alarm clock had awakened him, he turned on the radio and listened to music and when he had breakfasted and brushed his teeth, his dreams would be forgotten; the contact with his face was no longer an unpleasant experience, certainly no longer a frightening one, and he might even murmur tunelessly the words of some popular song as he shaved.

But on the morning following Faye's visit, he found his old face in the mirror; and though he did not realize it the summer happiness had ended. What remained was a series of events in which it would one day seem that reality had at some point merged with the world of his dreams.

On this morning Wesley awakened more tired than he had been at midnight. It was as if, lying on that bed with his eyes closed, he had performed some exhausting labour against profound obstacles. His back ached and there was a feeling of strain in his face and in the muscles of his jaws. Wesley knew even before he reached the mirror just what he would find there and so he avoided it for a long time.

Last night for the first time he could remember a dream had begun even before he was asleep and he had had to turn the light on before it would stop. In an effort to tire himself he had wandered through the streets until midnight and when at last he felt ready for sleep and had gone to bed, the trouble began: he thought he had heard a sound in the kitchen alcove and when he opened his eyes to look he saw the figure of a naked woman seated at the table staring at him. Even though he knew she was not a real person the clarity of her image frightened him. He sat up in bed and discovered that the woman was his mother. But she was not as he had remembered her, a proud overdressed bridge club president in a state of continuous activity, always putting on her hat, taking it off, preening herself like some bird in flight preparation, forever giddy, busy, endlessly chattering; the woman in the kitchen looked like his mother but her image had the transparency of a motion-picture ghost, she was naked and listless and sat staring at the bed with her finger poked into her own navel, scratching miserably. Her hair was a dry brown mass of lifeless wisps, and her face was bloodless and haggard, sad. There was no threat of violence in her presence but what made Wesley's fear grow almost to panic was the distinctness of her image, the exact reality of her every unreal aspect: in her pale eyes was the troubled look of one who is about to weep and in her posture was defeat, the distress of one on the brink of death.

In the morning, as Wesley sat drinking his coffee, he remembered that he had turned on the light and found no one but himself in the room; but for some time the clock had ticked with a menacing beat and for hours he had lain on the bed straining after sleep. Now, while Wesley was remembering, Earl appeared at the door. Wesley looked at him for a long time. At this moment he saw, in Earl, the flaw in his own life: the open door and the figure of an outsider who might at any moment enter.

Remembering what his life had been before the summer, he regretted each change he had permitted to come about. Inhabited as it may have been by obscure secrets and certain twisted dreams, his former invulnerability had at least precluded the entrance of new uninvited persons. Now he thought of Earl's first arrival several weeks ago and of his own strange willingness to accept the blind man; how Earl had managed, it now seemed, to appear at Wesley's door at just the proper psychological moment to win an invitation to a meal until, within so short a time, his presence at mealtime and at all times had become expected, had been taken for granted by both of them. He now attributed all of his unhappiness to this situation; and his own weakness in having permitted it to begin, and to persist, disgusted him.

Wesley vowed to himself to end this situation and to do it simply, quickly, without discussion. Earl had stood in the doorway for some minutes now and, watching him, Wesley remembered how, early in the summer, he had discovered that with Earl he could achieve solitude simply by remaining silent: perhaps this discovery would help him now.

When he had finished his coffee Wesley went to the door and though he had intended to say nothing, he paused and touched Earl's arm: "G'morning, There's coffee on the stove. I got to run. I'm late."

Whenever in his wanderings he heard the hum—which to others is a roar—of an aeroplane overhead, Earl Walker's hands remembered their contact with the wooden wings and twirling tin propeller of a toy he'd owned in childhood. But this was no decent substitute for seeing a real one take off or land or for watching it in its flight through that place known as the sky. Earl wanted to see, to be a person fit to enjoy movies, a sunrise, the distinction between night and day and the meaning of pink and hazel and bright green; and to see faces, those of people he knew and even those of strangers.

But this desire was not often in the foreground of his mind, for he knew that yearning after the impossible could make a madman of one who might otherwise be sane; say then that, inside of him, there was a small child insane with yearning for what he remembered of pine trees and snow, but Earl himself was a man and his life was not inhabited by faces. The world he lived in was one of sound and texture, of voices and the temperature of hands. Sight was outside of him, a satellite of his world, and he yearned for it only as some child on a summer evening might stare covetously at the moon.

Earl had been taught in a school for the blind to perform for himself all of the tasks necessary to existence; he could identify by touch or smell many objects which most sighted people have first to see. And in his twenty years of blindness and deafness he had developed some keen inner eye which could tell him the quality of the moods of others. When there were tensions he knew it as surely as if he had seen a frown wrinkle a brow or a lip tremble in anxiety or rage.

When he entered Wesley's apartment at breakfast time he knew some change had come about. He stood in the doorway for several minutes but he could hear no sound from within, only distant suggestions of sounds that could as well have been tricks in his own head. Then suddenly he felt a hand on his arm and he heard Wesley's voice:

"G'morning," Wesley said curtly, "there's coffee on the stove, I got to run. I'm late." Then Wesley brushed past him and Earl could hear him on the stairs.

Earl went to the stove and touched the coffee pot. It was hot. He went to the table and examined the cup and saucer and the position of the chair. And now he knew that Wesley had been sitting at the table and had seen him standing in the doorway but for some reason he had not spoken or given any signal at all.

6

Mrs. Kromer knew that the discomfort of the summer, the barely endurable heat, the impure air, was actually a blessing in disguise; these conditions were highly conducive to her meditations. For when the body suffers, the spirit is all the more willing to free itself. Each afternoon, when she had eaten her lunch of raw or lightly cooked vegetables (heavy foods and greases have a way of pasting the spirit on the body), she closed the doors and windows of her small parlour and drew the windowshades. Then, in semi-darkness, lying on her old wicker chaise longue in the centre of the room, she would close her eyes and concentrate on some imagined centre of light.

In this way, through pictures that appeared in this imagined light, she believed her life was guided from above. On certain days—all too often in fact—she saw the face of the Chinaman whom, by divine plan or perhaps through some great cosmic mistake, she had never met. He lived with a concubine who had borne him eleven sons. He was a good man but he found no happiness with this woman who was wrong for him in the first place and now, even though his skin was smooth and his hair as black as ever, Mrs. Kromer saw him as a very old man: his movements had become stiff and he had lost weight. Since all of his sons had left home to join the Communist army, he worked alone now and paused often in the fields to rest. The concubine, his woman, had grown fat and spent her days lolling about the house sucking on a piece of candied ginger. She offered him no comfort at all. Mrs. Kromer knew there was nothing she could do for him; both their present sojourns were nearly ended now and whenever his face appeared in her meditation, she would turn on the small lamp next to her chaise longue and read

Mrs. Barneweller until her mind had become freed once again.

"The world", according to Anna Hope Barneweller, "is a proving ground for sainthood, which is the common destiny of mankind." She taught that each man is born many times and that the soul of a man is the soul of God. "Severed from its Father at the time of its first birth, this spiritual entity begins its sojourn of thousands of years through multiple lifetimes until it has learned to transmute the pain of living into divine joy. All the sufferings of the body through afflictions and illnesses, and of the spirit in its essential loneliness, are designed to draw the soul of a man nearer and nearer to the end of its period of separation and darkness, closer and closer to God; and finally, having attained this purity through that final and joyful crucifixion to which each of us is destined, the entity once again rejoins the Soul of its Father in Heaven."

Now Mrs. Kromer knew a good deal about the entities who inhabited her building, especially those on the fourth floor. She had known the day Earl Walker arrived that he had been sent to teach Wesley Stuart a lesson. There had at that time been a vacancy in the second floor rear but Mrs. Kromer had chosen to assign him to the room that was likely to do the most good both for him and for Mr. Stuart. A blind man who could hardly even hear, one who had to go into the streets to sell leather goods, was a poor financial risk. Mrs. Kromer knew this, but she also knew that Christ, penniless as He was, would have been a certain sight poorer one. Would anyone in her right mind refuse to rent *Him a* room?

Events at first had gone along according to her expectations: Earl was taking his meals with Mr. Stuart and so far as she knew he wasn't paying anything for them. That was fine. All that money Mr. Stuart was making over in Hollywood had certainly done nobody's soul any good, not while it was sitting there stacked and glittering in some musty old bank vault.

This much, thanks be, had been simple: the blind man's food problem had been solved without any meditations at all. But this week, the third in a row, he had not paid his rent. Mrs. Kromer, lying with her eyes closed in the afternoon darkness, had been guided to silence in this issue. Then, last night, just as she had foreseen, Earl Walker had come to her of his own mind and explained that there were certain outstanding moneys owed him and he would be grateful for her patience in waiting for these to be paid up so that he in turn could cover his debt to her.

Now, the next day, Mrs. Kromer's mind had been burdened all morning long with the inhabitants of the fourth floor and by noon her stomach was so upset she had to refrain from eating any lunch at all. That little room of Earl's had gone unrented for a long time and she could manage well enough without the revenue from it, but the idea of Mr. Stuart just across the hall, his pockets as full as a handicapped race horse, weighing down the progress of his soul, disturbed her so seriously that one bite from a stalk of celery brought on a fearful attack of nausea and she had to spit it out at the garbage pail.

Instead of eating lunch, Mrs. Kromer turned out the lights and closed the doors to her parlour. But the windowshade offered resistance: each time she drew it in the blind snapped from her fingers, shot upward and, turning round and round at the top, flapped against the windowpane. Finally, standing barefoot on the sill, she flung a chenille bedspread over the curtain rod and, in a frenzy of urgency, hurried to the chaise longue.

She waited several minutes for her heart to stop pounding but even before her eyes were closed the light appeared like a tiny sun and, after a moment or two, her course was set.

That evening Wesley, who had decided that a few days' withdrawal from his problems would bring about the best solution to them, went for a long drive in the San Fernando Valley and took his dinner alone at a quiet little roadhouse where soft delicate sounds were piped in from some unseen piano. This was his first dinner alone since the summer had begun; it was pleasant and he ate slowly.

Later, when he arrived at his apartment, Earl was nowhere in sight and it was evident that the blind man had not been here during the day, not even for lunch. Wesley was pleased with this progress he had made in readjusting his life.

He closed the door and sat down to inspect the contents of an envelope that had been addressed to him in Mrs. Kromer's handwriting and shoved under his door.

Dear Mr. Stuart,

It has been my meaning to catch you in the halls for a good while now to thank you for something principally your kindness to Mister Walker whose eyes the Lord has seen fit to seal as well as his left ear and a part of the right one. This food he gets from you is a blessing and there is only left one problem to devil him. He frets to me about the rent bill in the amount of twenty-four dollars and such a shame for a piddling little bit of filthy lucre but I tell him dont fret son as the Lord is a tender shepherd and will find a way just as he found a way to feed you. God bless you from your friend and confident.

Miranda Kromer.

P.S. I hope your nightmares are no longer so bad but when they act up be sure I will welcome to interprate again at any time.

Wesley was irritated but only for a moment. The artlessness of the note amused him. He wondered how long Mrs. Kromer must have laboured to achieve even this degree of subtlety. He imagined her in her parlour on the first floor, pacing back and forth in a beltless housedress, a stub of a pencil in one hand, a fly swatter in the other, straightening a throw-rug with her big knuckled foot, planning, calculating the effect of her words; and how, finally, her huge and wild eyes ablaze with inspiration, she had leaned over the kitchen table and begun; then, after a dozen or more false starts, while the perspiration gleamed on her forehead, she had discarded one version after another until at last, in one fine masterful stroke, she had come upon this final one that would surely produce the perfect result.

For three days Wesley did not encounter the blind man anywhere but he thought of him often and wondered where he was taking his meals. These thoughts disturbed him but he knew that sooner or later he would forget about Earl; it took time to repair the damage caused by certain errors, lapses in strength, and he went about his living and doing, alone as before, waiting patiently for the return of his contentedness. He busied himself with his car, cleaning and washing it, making minor repairs, taking long drives into the mountains and through the valleys; and with going to movies and discovering new and interesting places to eat. He did not enjoy his solitude any more, but he was certain that within a short time he would regain the sense of delight he had once felt in the company of himself. He planned to spend a week-end in

San Francisco; new surroundings would command his attention.

That Friday evening, after work, he and the car were on Sunset Boulevard headed toward the ocean. He drove for a long time and soon the ocean was on his left and then he turned on the radio, volume high, and let this jazz music blare out against the sounds of the sea. For a while the palisades were on his right and then he came to Malibu and slowed down, perhaps to stop; he was hungry but he did not feel like eating. He drove for another longer time until the sun had set and his hunger no longer bothered him and soon it was as if he had become a part of the car, its motor and the jazz. His thoughts were not those of a person but of things, machines and oceans, rhythms, and all their noises were a part of him so that the time and the space he covered were like nothing and ceased to exist or to have meanings. He drove for a long time.

Now the headlights illuminated briefly some white object, a cat, a rabbit, a bird—there was no telling, it happened too quickly. As it connected with the bumper there was a quick soft thump and Wesley began to tremble; his thinking had begun again and he had no control over it. In his mind the white object crushed against the car took shape again until it grew and had become a person; and Wesley was terrified by a sudden wondering whether this drive tonight were not a drive to death. But the obvious absurdity of the notion comforted him. He realized that his own irrational guilt at having deserted a man who might be hungry—irrational because he could in no way be responsible to a stranger—had conspired against him just as Mrs. Kromer and Earl himself had done.

He stopped at a filling station and turned off the motor. The radio stopped playing at the same instant and this new silence was as lovely as the noise had once been: a silence composed of softer rhythms, more distant sounds, the sea, his voice and the voice of the station attendant. He walked around to the front of the car to examine the bumper and found it splattered with blood. Dark red spots had dried on the metal strips of the grill.

Wesley asked for the rest-room and he was directed to a small white room where there was a sink, a toilet and a mirror with the word SANITARY in red cellophane letters glued over its surface.

He looked into the mirror and found his morning face: the red-rimmed empty eyes reflecting the hunger of a man much older, the wasted despair of some ancient prospector who had spent his life in search of gold on a desert where there was nothing but sand. The night wind and earlier the sun had dried his skin and now in the mirror he could see certain lines that had never been there before. His lips seemed separate from the rest of him, as if large frozen berries had been stuck into the face of a corpse. Wesley felt a nausea come upon him which he believed had resulted from his long abstinence from food. He leaned over the toilet and stuck his finger into his throat but nothing came out but air, a deep prolonged belch that brought with it an absurd echo as if the sound had been produced from the depths of some great empty cavern.

Instead of continuing northward he returned to Pasadena. It was long past midnight when he arrived. He sat at the table and wrote a cheque for twenty-four dollars and then he wrote a brief note to Mrs. Kromer in which he said he liked being left alone and would appreciate her co-operation in seeing to it that no one annoyed him with gratitude. When he had placed the envelope under her door, he climbed the stairs once more and, leaving the door to his apartment open several inches to permit the entrance of air from the hallway, he went to bed. Within a moment or two, Wesley was asleep.

7

People in the San Gabriel Valley do not as a rule pray for rain to relieve the summer heat; they pray for a certain wind from the Pacific to find its way in through the barriers of mountains all around. On this night, in the August of this summer, such a wind arrived and the next morning the sky was blue, the rays of the sun were gentle rays, and in Pasadena you could see people working in their gardens pruning rose trees or picking those plums that had not gone rotten on the branches. There was a midsummer renewal of life as if some lovely freak spring had taken place on a desert.

Wesley awakened to the smell of coffee and to the sounds of the percolator. The windowshades were still drawn but when he opened his eyes he saw a shadow moving about in the kitchen. But because he knew who it was, Wesley was not alarmed.

The good night wind had had the effect of a stimulating drug breathed into the valley's air by some great wizard: the season's stillness gave place to activity. Mrs. Kromer put on a pair of bright blue ankle socks and stepped into her shoes—gentlemen's sport shoes with crepe soles— and walked over to Marengo Avenue where for the first time in many weeks she did her own marketing. Wesley Stuart drove his car into the driveway and with a cool stream of water from a long black garden hose he washed his car in the shadow of the house. Miss Faye Zelger returned laden with parcels from a dime-store shopping spree at about 11 a.m. She stopped for a moment in the driveway to comment on the loveliness of the weather and Wesley was struck so by the new sobriety of her manner, a quality of almost genuine sweetness, that he decided to give her a civil answer. Then Faye walked away singing, using lalala instead of words, into the house. Wesley covered the car with some white liquid mud from a bottle and then with cheesecloth he set about removing it, polishing vigorously until soon the car shone like a black mirror and he parked it once again on the street.

Now Mrs. Kromer and Earl Walker appeared at the corner, walking toward the house. Under her left arm she carried a carton of fresh vegetables and her right arm was looped through Earl's. She walked with difficulty as if there were hot coals underfoot, for even in these over-sized gentlemen's shoes, her huge old feet yearned for freedom. Earl carried a large bunch of gladioli given him by an overstocked florist on Green Street.

Some minutes later Wesley and Earl climbed into the shining car and drove to the beach. Mrs. Kromer took the flowers into her kitchen and when she had arranged them in three glass milk bottles, each with the words 3 cents DEPOSIT stamped in orange on the sides, she kicked off her shoes and delivered two of the bouquets—one to Faye across the hall and the second to Wesley's kitchen table on the fourth floor.

Wesley and Earl returned from the beach late in the afternoon. They stopped at a supermarket where Wesley purchased two large bagfuls of groceries and later, with appetites sharpened by the good sea air and a long afternoon of walking on the drenched sand at the ocean's edge, these two men sat down to a meal of broiled beef that was black on the outside and red in the middle, broccoli, dark bread, strawberries and milk, and when they had drunk some coffee and smoked a couple of cigarettes, Earl said he had places to go and things to do later in the evening. Wesley believed this activity had something to do with the earning of the blind man's livelihood and even though at some point in the last twenty-four hours he had decided to continue his association with Earl, it was not his intention to discourage any man's efforts to gain his independence.

When Earl had left the house Wesley cleaned his apartment, a job which had been neglected for several days, and after he had taken a warm bath and then a cool one, he lay on his bed contented, pleased that the strangeness had once again ascended from the world, had retreated to those unknown areas of the sky, where with all the other demons Mrs. Kromer spoke of, those that really did seem to stalk about the earth causing disease in a man's peace, they truly belonged.

Though he was relaxed and there was peace inside of him now for the first time in days, he did not yet feel ready for sleep; and so he searched about for something to read and came upon a volume that had been given to him a long time ago. It was called *A Primer for Sainthood*, and its author was Mrs. Anna Hope Barneweller. He thought, with sympathy now, of Mrs. Kromer, and as he sat on the bed, smiling, he turned back the cover of the book.

One afternoon in early September Mrs. Kromer stopped Earl Walker on the stairs and told him that if he would kindly step into her parlour she would conduct some important business with him.

When they were seated, she said, "What colour's the sky today, young fella?" Earl said he thought it was probably blue and Mrs. Kromer told him he was exactly correct and in case he wondered, blue was the colour of a cool glass of water splashed in your face on a hot day. Then she said, "Earl I am privileged to tell you some good news. You have got a secret benefactor interested in your welfare."

Earl sat forward in his chair. "A secret what?"

"Benefactor, honey. A benefactor is a good person that likes to help out."

"Who?"

"That's what's secret. I have no liberty to tell."

She brought out a pad of paper and a pencil and sat down, facing him. "All you got to do is give me a list of what money you owe various folks and I take it to this secret person."

Earl thought for a moment. "And I won't even know who it is, ever?"

"It's God, mister, that's all you got to know. Everything good comes from God. That blue sky, the cool water, the whole works. Now let's tend to business."

Earl Walker and Mrs. Kromer sat at that table for a long time, thinking, figuring, scratching out certain items—she thought the seventy-five cents to Mr. Stokes at the coffee place was not big enough to trouble over—and replacing them with others, discussing this sudden good fortune; and when Mrs. Kromer totalled the figures they came to more than three hundred dollars. Earl wondered if this benefactor could afford all that and Mrs. Kromer reassured him.

"Earl," she said, "I want to remind you that God's source of supply stretches from here to Hongkong and then it keeps on goin'."

"I was wondering", Earl said, "if I could put down a debt I haven't got yet. One I'll have in about a week."

"Anything at all," Mrs. Kromer said, "anything to help lighten the burden from your darkness. How much?"

"A hundred and eight dollars."

Mrs. Kromer added that to the rest. "That's a fancy figure, brother," she said. "You fixin' to buy a house?"

Earl smiled with happiness and his eyes were as bright as if the pictures in them contained all the beautiful colours and shapes in the world.

"Nope. No house," he said.

That evening, after dinner on the fourth floor, something happened which in itself is a natural thing to happen but which to Wesley, later in his life when he would think about it, was strange, unforgettable.

Earl suddenly asked him what he looked like.

"Oh, just uh—you know, like anybody else, Earl."

Earl had embarrassed himself but his curiosity forced him to pursue the question. "You can't look like *any*body else."

"You'd be surprised. I'm just as average as a...Well, I'm sorry, Earl, I guess I don't know how to describe myself."

"Mrs. Kromer told me you were about my height and she said you had gold hair. Do you?"

"Sometimes it looks gold, but it's just blond."

Earl laughed a forced laugh that was intended to relieve his discomfiture but only succeeded in increasing it. "I thought only girls had blonde hair." He was quiet for a moment and then, with sudden decision, he said, "Wesley, I'm going to ask you something and you tell me yes or no and then forget it. Okay?"

"Okay."

"There's only one way I know how somebody looks and that's if I touch his face. D'you mind?"

After a moment, Wesley reached across the small table; he took Earl's hand and, leaning forward, he guided this hand to his face. For a brief moment this smooth open palm rested against his cheek and then suddenly the fingers, infinitely gentle, began quickly to explore his face, stopping now and again as if to memorize what they had found. Wesley thought he had never experienced such profound tenderness, and because he was trembling, he gripped the table firmly to prevent Earl from detecting his emotion. Wesley had learned to find in the movement of

Earl's hands all that might be found in the eyes of a person with sight; and now when Earl's hand hesitated for a moment he knew that during this pause some knowledge was being registered in the blind man's brain.

Earl's touch lingered for a moment at the corner of Wesley's eye and then he took his hand from Wesley's face and quickly rubbed the forefinger against the thumb, causing a tear to evaporate on the skin. Then Earl took hold of a bunch of Wesley's hair and gently pulled it. "You got a good face," he said.

Earl removed the napkin from his lap, rose from the table, excused himself and left the room. Wesley walked over to the door and closed it. Then he lay down on the bed and dropped a soft white pillow on to his face.

8

Though September was a hot month the winds had driven the smog away and one could enjoy once again the outdoors, breathe good air and observe in comfort the progress of late summer flowers. The sun, now a warming and illuminating thing, decorating the valley in light and shadow, had ceased to create a glare.

For several days Wesley saw Earl only at mealtime. Earl said he had hit a streak of luck in the sale of his leather goods and each day after dinner he left with unusual abruptness and Wesley spent the evenings alone. But he looked forward to the week-ends when he and Earl often took long drives into the mountains and to the beach. On these trips Wesley would often describe their surroundings and sometimes they would get out of the car and walk for a long time and eat a packed lunch in the open country. As the week grew to a close Wesley's anticipation grew and he marked time like a child waiting for Christmas.

One Friday night he had a dream: he and Earl Walker were on the lawn in front of Mrs. Kromer's house and they were building an aeroplane. In this dream Earl was no longer blind and he took an active part in the construction. Now this dream-plane was like none that has ever been seen: it had two fuselages crossed in the middle, and no wings at all, only these two crossed bodies forming a great letter X, and two propellers, one facing east and the other south. Wesley, dreaming, saw himself and Earl climb into the cockpit. The plane began to climb, straight up like a helicopter, and when it had risen higher than the house, this strange aircraft went into a nosedive and crashed on the lawn. Wesley saw Earl climb unharmed from the plane; but he himself was slumped dead in the cockpit. Mrs. Kromer hurried down the porch steps and laid her hand on Wesley's shoulder, and in a voice of command she said, *"Those who are dead will come to life."* Then, obediently, he arose.

That was the end of the dream. But even after he had awakened Wesley could hear those words echoing in him. He remembered each detail of the dream and turned them over and over in his mind. Even though their meanings were not entirely clear the dream itself seemed to prophesy some new life, perhaps one which had already begun.

His thoughts turned to the room across the hall, that eternally dark place in which sound itself was seldom more than the hum and rhythm of distant things and in which there were no colours but imagined ones, no shapes but those that could be remembered in the fingertips: and he imagined that if people really did have souls as Mrs. Barneweller's book indicated—and they certainly must, because she had *proven*, it seemed to him now, that dreams themselves were some fragment of the soul's activity—then Earl must surely have a simple and beautiful one, contained as it was within the tranquil shell of his dark and silent life where peace, like geometry, must reign even in sleep.

He lay for a long time reviewing these quiet and golden thoughts and then drifted again into sleep. When he awakened the sun was shining through the drawn curtains. Suddenly he realized that today was Saturday. He dressed quickly, brushed his teeth, and lighted a fire under the tea kettle. He drew back the curtains and let the sun come in and then he opened the door so that Earl would know he was awake.

By nine o'clock he had shaved, swept the floors, and prepared breakfast. Anxious to begin the week-end, he crossed the hall and knocked on Earl's door. There was no response and he knocked again, this time with his fist.

At last he heard a stirring from within. Satisfied that Earl had awakened, he turned to leave. But just as he stepped inside his own room, he heard a door open and a voice speaking to him in a whisper.

"D'you knock on our door, Wesley?"

Still half asleep, her body partly covered by a green kimono held imperfectly together by one hand at the waist, Faye Zelger stood at Earl Walker's door. A patch of nakedness showed under the torn armpit of her gown and the pink nipple of one tiny breast was exposed. With her free hand she rubbed sleep from an eye and pushed a long lock of hair from her face; then, hushing him with a gesture, she closed Earl's door behind her and, to Wesley, she said, "What you want, dear?"

Wesley stared at her incredulously as she moved toward him in the hall.

"You boys have some date or other? We got t'bed s'late, I just thought t'hell with the alarm clock. An' we've got this fearful trip ahead of us." Wesley's lips were parted and he continued to stare at her. "Well," she continued, "don't look s'stupid, honey. Didn't you *know?* We'uns 're goin' t'Flahrida t'night,"

Her dialect seemed to Wesley even broader than before, and her manner stung him almost as sharply as the knowledge it conveyed. He tried to speak but it took a moment to form the word, "Tonight?"

Faye flung her hands into the air like a mimic acting out the word hopeless. "Lawurd, he hasn't told you a thang! He just *despises* conversation. But all sorts o'things bin happenin', Wesley. Mamma's bin beggin' me t'come home and promises to b'have herself. I wrote her the whole shebang—eyes, hearing aid, ever'thing. But Mamma says 'Bring 'im on ahead.' I think she's lonesome. Anyhow we're takin' the eleven-oh-two."

Faye folded her arms over her breasts and took a step forward; then, looking directly and, it seemed to him, with a certain calculated boldness into his eyes, she said, "Wesley, there's one part absolutely secret and I know you're not the kind t'tell, so listen." She blinked her eyes and licked the morning dryness from her lips. "Our bus tickets", she said, "were taken care of by a secret *benefactor"*

Perhaps if Faye had turned away, what followed might never have happened. But she continued to look into Wesley's eyes.

Wesley's open palm shot forward and lifted the girl into the air. She landed with a hard smack on the floor and screamed. Then, bending over her, he filled his left hand with her hair and beat her across the face several times with his open palm. Faye's voice was now trapped inside of her and she was no longer able to scream.

Wesley stood back and looked at Faye as she huddled close to the floor, fixed by fear, holding her face in her hands. Blood appeared between her fingers and mingled with her hair. Then the door opened and Earl, smiling in his ignorance stood there naked with his head cocked to one side trying to listen. He held out his hand and said, "Hey, where *is* everybody?"

Now Faye scrambled over to him on the floor and threw her arms about his legs and a sudden deep frown creased Earl's face and his sightless toy-doll eyes opened wide: "Faye?" He touched the top of her head with his fingertips. Faye began at that moment to sob hysterically and Wesley saw some insane dream image of himself on the floor in a bloody green kimono clinging to the blind man's ankles. He turned quickly to his own door and closed it behind him.

There was a click of a key turning in his lock.

Summoned by a third-floor tenant, Mrs. Kromer appeared, breathless, her heart pounding hard inside of her. Faye tried to tell her what had happened but she had lost some of her powers of articulation: "He's lost his mind, he's lost his mind!" Faye repeated this over and over again and Mrs. Kromer guided these two people to her parlour on the first floor and after she had bathed Faye's swollen and still swelling face and told Earl not to worry, she ran barefooted all the way to the top of the house, not even hearing the questions hurled at her by tenants along the way and ignoring completely a warning that a woman her age should not run up and down the stairs like a twelve-year-old. She knocked on Wesley's door. She knocked for a long time but there was no response.

"Mr. Stuart?" she called softly. "Mr. Stuart? Can you hear me?" She paid no attention to a long sharp pain that began somewhere in her chest and travelled through her left arm and into her head; because almost as soon as it began, the pain ceased, and whole parts of her became numb. With her ear pressed against the keyhole she listened for another moment but there was no sign of life within. Then, her own vertigo mounting with each word, she spoke softly into that keyhole: "Mr. Stuart?" she said. "Can you still hear me? Can you still hear my voice?"

Half an hour later in front of Wesley's door where several of the tenants had assembled, it was generally believed that their landlady had known, had had sufficient warning that death was near, and had taken the time to arrange herself comfortably on the floor. One bare foot pointed west and the other east. Her face had turned blue but she was smiling an eyeless open-mouthed greeting to the sun that now streamed through the skylight.

Inside the locked door, Wesley lay on the bed with his eyes closed. Of the sounds that reached him, only these had meaning: dead died passed away poor soul—and, appropriately, he placed his left hand over his heart and crossed it with his right.

The Jazz of Angels

When she walks west along the Boulevard, into the setting sun, Lizzie Ballinet is coming from her studio. The studio has been boarded up for a number of years but in its heyday Lizzie appeared in upward of two hundred crowd scenes giving what she called "cameo" performances and between takes read tealeaves for forty-three big stars, predicting accurately an astonishing number of divorces and marriages and suppressing the clairvoyant knowledge of several headlined deaths including two suicides and a murder. These statistics are recorded by her in a five-year diary, a 1932 Christmas present from Russ Colombo which she carries in a gold net shopping bag during her traipses up and down Hollywood Boulevard. Her studio is boarded up now but Lizzie reports anyway to the front gate each day as a matter of discipline and continues to exercise her special seeing powers in order to avoid being driven by idleness into the role of a Hollywood Character, a fate considered by her to be far worse than mere unemployment.

When Lizzie Ballinet moves along the Boulevard in no straight line she is an object to stare at and think about. This is why: she wears on the outside what most people wear on the inside.

Most of what she sees is behind her eyes and not reflected in them. Another pedestrian will often hesitate in the face of that blue saucer stare, and say "I beg your pardon" to avoid a collision; then Lizzie will detain him with a monologue: "There was some reason for you speaking to me, sir, it was no accident. No accident that out of all these people you chose me! If there's any way under the heavens you can take a trip, then take it. You're either happy or unhappy, one can't be two things at once, and this is a three vibration—*time to travel!* Go along if you must but remember what I say, remember me, never forget the lovely lady who spoke to you on Hollywood Boulevard."

Lizzie's eyes are of the china blue remembered from a special candy dish or lamp base in some antique dealer's windowcase and they are glossy with perpetual tears. Lizzie likes the tears; in fact she cultivates them. They help to obscure the undesirable and even tend to paint a silvery sheen on grime. They alter her focus so that there is never one of an object, but always two, three or none. None is usually the number of unpleasant things, unshaven gentlemen, necks without ties, or smiles that are not intended to be kind. The tears are one of a series of artifices Lizzie uses to muffle her senses.

Her hair is real but it has to be pinned on every morning and sent to the beauty parlour each week, sometimes with, sometimes without Lizzie. A picture hat secured by ribbons tied under the chin keeps her hair in place; from its wide brim hangs a network of heavy sky-blue threads. This nose-veil, along with the tears, keeps her from seeing the ten thousand inter-connecting lines on her face; and this is well for she does not remember clearly the ten thousand stories they represent.

One of them returns to her now and then in fragments: a strawberry patch, late twilight, Nebraska, a blue shirt and twilight arms, the Angelus bell ringing, strawberry lips and the taste of salt—but it returns with no more specific meaning than that the images of earth and water and flesh and light and a faceless man named Adam denote the beginning of the world.

When the music of a jazz band emanating from a cocktail bar along the Boulevard reaches her ears it somehow keeps going inside of her, fills her body and excludes everything else. Three or four bars of this blue rhythm are enough to transform the street into a garden party. Lizzie begins to dance and there are people who stop and watch, some laughing, pointing her out, others jeering and applauding; and there are even a few who stand with quiet reverence in the face of this projection of the secret life of another. There are remarks and automobile horns and police whistles—but these noises find no mark in Lizzie's mind; they mingle with the jazz and soon the medley comes to an end with one strong ensemble break.

Lizzie moves along.

She stops at a news-stand to ask for a magazine that has not been printed for several decades and begins talking to the clerk:

"A wonderful thing happens to your mouth: the ends turn up. *Up*, do you hear? You've a high forehead, you're a born philosopher, but you're no go-getter. Everyone can't be and there's room for you, too. *My* type makes the best automobile driver but we're not much good at anything else. How old would you say I was to look at me; I have the body of an adolescent, my doctor says it's abnormal. We were meant to meet like this, it was all intended, you with your lovely eyes and me with my adolescent body. If you come home with me tonight I'll open a bottle of champagne!

"What makes the ends of your mouth turn *up* so? What'd you say? Never mind repeating it, I don't hear anyway. A-ha-haa-haaa! Bless you, dear! Magazines,

magazines! I don't like reading, it's mostly lies you know. Good night. Forget me if you can!"

Lizzie has not been rejected; she feels the young man's eyes caressing her figure as it moves along the Boulevard; there are bound to be certain magazines one does not carry, that one must say no to—such a bright young turning-up at the corners of the mouth!

She pauses for a moment, and looks back: "Forget the *moon*, forget the corner of Hollywood and *Vine*, the colour of the sky and *who you are!* Forget the first time you kissed some pretty little lady! But I promise you," she shouts, "you'll never forget Lizzie Ballinet! B-a-l-l-i-n-e-t, Ballinet! The lady who made you blush from the hairline to the collar! Don't frown, young man, you'll wrinkle yourself early!" She sends a kiss travelling on the air toward him, and turns away, chastising herself gently: "Shame on you, Lizzie. Coquetry is a crime in the springtime, a-ha-haa-haaaa!"

Pain! Her pace slackens.

Pain, spurting down the length of her back. She is on a darker street, carrying her shoes, and the sidewalk under her stockinged feet is damp and a little too cold. The streetlight looks like white ice. It takes the temperature of many bodies and the noises of crowds to warm a sidewalk. It takes ...to sustain a springtime attitude, it takes ...! "Now, Lizzie," she chides herself, "you're faltering! Quickly, Lizzie, look up your advice to Miss D. Something about transmute, transmutation, trans-*some*thing." She hurries to the streetlight and reaches into her shopping bag. "Hurry now! The Colombo volume, try 1936—spring! Here: 'Dear Miss D.,' " she reads, aloud, " 'Do not accept ugliness, do not accept time. Every man, every woman and child is an alchemist. He has the power to turn pain into pleasure, aloneness into love. Baser metals like death are simply there to be transmuted.' Yes, the word was trans*muted*."

The pain subsides. Lizzie moves along, remembering aloud: "Poor, frightened, *mis*erable Miss D. We were shooting the drugstore sequence on Stage 9, one of my finest moments on film—or *would* have been if poor Miss D. hadn't been tricked; *tricked* into believing she was old and broken and sick and alone. Then of course the attack was inevitable. Death on a movie set. Out*rag*eous! I said, 'Dear Miss D., if you can't make believe *here*, where can you?' Then the poor thing died and the director said, 'Goddamit, when we hire one of these old bitches, we ought to give 'em a complete goddam *physical* before we shoot a goddam foot o' film.' Ha-haa-haaa! Poor man! I must go home and look up my advice to Mr. V."

There is a dark building standing before her. She watches, dry-eyed now, the still reflections of the street lamp on the panes of glass. "Dear Miss D.," she says, addressing the dark house, "you complain that you live alone. You say there is no light behind the window, no *man* waiting for you. Very well. But isn't there a dog or a cat, a child or a mouse? Very well, Miss D., now tell me there are no *other* resources! No transmutation possible! I refuse to preach..."

A tiny ice-cream truck rolls slowly down the middle of the street. Its chimes play Yankee-doodle, over and over again—stuck a feather in his hat and called it macaroni! Now: Yankee-doodle went to town...

Lizzie stops the truck.

"Ice-cream man! Stop, ice-cream man!"

The chimes stop playing while a sale is being made but their sounds have already warmed her.

"This is the most beautiful night of my life. You and your white charger full of ice-cream! I'd like the kind with chocolate coating on a little wooden stick." She fumbles with her purse. "Whoever invented pocket-books? You never find a thing in them, much less a dime. I'll ride around the block with you a few times till I've found it. I'll bring you luck. All my friends love me and they eat ice-cream all the time. —Well, just to the next corner? Never mind, dear, here's a quarter. No no no, you *keep* that, all for yourself. A-ha-haa-haaa! Yes, all for you! Good night, my dear good sweet prince!"

Yankee-doodle went to town a-riding on a pony, stuck a feather in his hat and turned a little cor-ner!

A-ha-haaa!

A little cor-ner. The street is dark again and the ice-cream is cold. But the chimes keep going around the corner and inside of her. She moves toward the door like a dark-town strutter arriving at the ball. It helps to dance and hear music when you turn the key and open the door to an empty house, it helps when the walls rattle so inside your mind to hear music and to dance.

Lizzie flips a switch but no electric current can squelch all that darkness.

"Come to life, darlings! Lizzie's home from her studio. Another union meeting today; the membership is trying to *force* her into the presidency, but there's simply no time, no time. There is no time—left! Eat this ice-cream, quickly, right away, dear prince, it's melting fast!"

She lays the gift on top of the radio, then turns the switch and spins the dial all the way to the right.

"What shall we talk about tonight? Now I don't want to hear one word about war, just play some soothing music and then we'll sleep. If you knew how tired I..."

There is a series of removals : a hat, a wig, a coat, a dress, a petticoat, a pair of panties, a brassiere, a pair of stockings. Then she hears the man's voice:

"If you're like most people you prefer *fresh* orange juice, you like to squeeze it yourself and get all the *real goodness* and value that nature intended for you. But it isn't always possible, is it? You don't always have *time*. Not when you're *rushing* to keep an appointment, when you're hurrying to get Johnnie off to school on time. Now I want to tell you about a product that com*bines*..."

Lizzie stands before the mirror talking to the voice. Tear-filled eyes cling to the reflection. "You are whimsical, my dear, whimsical, no other word. I have the body of an adolescent, a-ha-haaa, and you talk about orange juice."

The man spins a record for Lizzie. The first few movements of her dance are performed at the mirror but soon she is drawn to his Afro-Cuban heartbeat, the ice-cream is melting, the hips are swaying and deep inside her body pain like ice spreads its cold venom and fills her.

"Da-dum-de-a-da-DEE, Da-dum-de-a-da-DA! No no no, not another word about orange juice, you precious fool!"

She spins the dial. For one terrible moment of static silence the man is so much wood and electricity; the cold snake of pain begins to steal in between the creaking rafters of her mind.

"The beautiful Swan Lake Casino brings you the music of Claude Wakefield, music in the danceable Wakefield manner! We're dancing under the stars tonight and every night until two in the magical setting of Paradise. Swan Lake Casino, located three miles from Malibu along the Pacific coast..."

"But my darling, if you knew what a day I've had. We shot the drugstore sequence and Miss D. died on Stage 9. No of course I'm not tired, I'm never ever tired, but I do get sleepy, so very ...very..."

Lizzie turns out the light and climbs into bed.

"Don't go *on* so about it, we'll go dancing tomorrow. Now, maestro, darling, play something soothing while I think what to say to Miss D. A concerto with lots of fiddles, one of those dream-like Sibelius things I love so."

But Sibelius does not know about the Swan Lake Casino. There they have a bass fiddle, a piano and a set of drums, a clarinet, a trumpet and trombone, and these six instruments and the fingers and lips of the players, with nothing in common but a Paradise drinking spot located some miles from Malibu on the Pacific coast and a certain chaotic rhythm dictated by the time of their lives, send sounds across the airwaves that will never be heard again. The melted ice-cream trickles down the front of the radio leaving the dial sticky with chocolate. Lizzie's aching body lies naked on the bed.

"A-ha-haa-haaa! This is much more exciting than Sibelius. Now crawl into bed, dear, I've had a trying, trying...Ooooh! Darling, your *hands*, they're ice! Put them here, here between ...there now, that's better. There!"

Even with Claude Wakefield's danceable music filling the room, a dangerous silence lies next to Lizzie, a silence which must be transmuted. The workings of her adolescent heart have been slowed by pain.

How to transmute the silence that lies next to one in springtime when sleep will not come quickly enough to fill one with old-fashioned images of berry patches before the pain takes hold!

"Dear heart, can you reach me my Colombo volume? It's there in my—quickly, dear, I've got to . . .!"

Six live angels come to the rescue pushing their hearts into percussion and Gabriel horns all the way from Swan Lake Casino and now the transmutation of silence is no longer in the hands of Lizzie. They reach out far, they reach out to heaven with their pulses and the time of their lives in common, they cling to the gates with quivering fingers on goatskin and ivory and brass.—And the twilight long-ago arms surround her as softly as light falling on a new earth.

I love you, my beautiful Lizzie, I love you I love you I love you.

The music stops, but only for a moment. There is a change of tempo.

Pretty on the Bus at Night-time

You know yourself it is no treat watching a fat lady weep and it was for this reason I tried to cure myself. I did like a doctor getting after a disease: he looks for the cause and then he nips the thing in the roots.

I turned the facts over carefully in my head and came up with the idea I needed another husband was the trouble with me. It had been three years since Hugo got into my Ford and drove away.

My Ford.

That's the way it was. He was a brave, reckless, generous, hard-drinking type of a man but I had to do the paying for it. We spent seven years married and during that time he worked three weeks. Three weeks which almost killed him, he said. Hugo was a big, good-looking type of a man which wants a free ride out of life with his wife in the driver's seat but I don't want to go into all that again. Leave it sufficed to say a woman's got to be a wife and not a husband; sometimes she can be a husband but not if she's got to be a wife at the same time. Let us leave it sufficed to say that.

I examined the cause for the weepiness in this doctor-like way and came up with the idea I needed another husband, a real one to be preferred please, no more nothings thanks. That is when I thought of doing the thing I don't brag about, which is namely writing a letter to the ad in the paper. Nothing ever came of it because I couldn't tell the truth in the letter; it looks all right in the flesh when it's dressed up wearing lipstick and all, but on paper the truth is not too inviting.

There was no way you could word it.

"Dear Sir, I am a lady alone. I have a good disposition and collect as a hobby the poems of Mr. Guest from the daily paper pasting them in a scrap-book which I made and decorated myself. (The ad said he liked poetry.) I have a lovely daughter Melody aged six who is also the daughter of a husband which I divorced some time ago because of certain reasons. I am between 30 and 40 as you specify and am considered pretty even though a little chubby..."

I crossed out chubby and put pleasingly plump, I crossed out pleasingly plump and put overweight, then I put quite fat as a matter of fact, sir, then I tore up the damn letter and said to hell with you, Mr. Dear Sir.

And then I wept some.

It takes more than writing a letter to cure you. For weepiness is a dreadful sickness which I had a serious case of. Writing a letter only picks at the scab. You might as well put a shot of penicillin in the ocean to cure it from being deep.

Last spring things came to a head.

I had been working nights cleaning out doctors' offices. It was my job to dust and straighten up the magazines you look through waiting for your appointment and I swept the floors, mopping them well twice a week. Doctors' offices don't get too dirty except for bandages in the waste-basket and medicine spilled here and there. The best thing was being all alone and you could sit down and think, or even once in a while I have been known to take a short nap.

In the daytime I took care of my little girl Melody who in the night-time stayed next door with the lady from the church. I would say Melody is an angel but I am not the kind of mother who says such things of her child. Say she is sweet and pretty and does not look at all like she is going to be fat; say that much and leave it be.

I took care of her in the daytime and did other things in between like sleeping and washing the clothes and collecting the rent from the tenant upstairs. Because of being a landlady there were books to keep and payments to make on the house, something keeping you at it every minute.

The day things came to a head I was doing the weekly wash on the back porch, feeling worse than a sick horse what with a bad headache caused by the shots which are supposed to make you slim and not much sleep to boot; add that up and plenty of work not done, three letters in window envelopes waiting in the mailbox which I was afraid to open because of knowing good and well they were bills. Then Melody started screaming her blonde little head off in the yard.

I looked up to see what she'd fallen into and my hand started running through the wringer. It was up past my wrist before I had the good sense to pull the switch which gets you out of trouble in such cases. I kept on with the washing until my hand started to burn with the pain all the way up to the elbow and felt like there was not one good bone left in it.

I have said to myself a thousand times, Irene don't weep, but this is no help. Neither is nothing else. Even getting mad is no better. I rested my head on the washing machine for one good weeping fest and the next thing I knew my hair was feeding itself to that blessed wringer.

I was half scalped before my hand pulled the switch again.

I remember sitting down in the middle of the floor with fuzzy thoughts going through my head knowing the mess is too much now to cope with it alone. The wet-wash in the basket was splashed over with blood. The sky was an ornery quiet blue. There was a scream that must have come from me.

Some time later I was in bed and sitting next to me was Mrs. Krangsprush, the lady from the church, telling me about positive thoughts. She had a theory it was the devil pushed my hair through that wringer but I knew I had done it myself without his help. The doctor told Mrs. K. I was not seriously scalped but should take things slow and easy for a few weeks and keep away from the washing machine till my mind was cleared up from the worry.

Melody sat at the foot of the bed looking big-eyed and scared as a rabbit in a trap.

"Your mamma's all right, Melody," I said giving her a kiss and a squeeze along with it. Mrs. Krangsprush took over Melody and the house duties while I stood in bed for a few weeks, and what with the tenant, Mrs. Bruce, bringing down soup and Boston beans and other things to help out, I laid there getting a helluva good rest and a new bird's-eye view on things about life. Things like all the sleep I could hold and the two kind neighbour-ladies solving the daily problems.

Melody, too.

She brought me a bouquet from my old-fashioned garden. A few of the flowers had roots hanging on the ends of them but you don't bawl a little child out when they're giving you a gift. We talked flowers, I not knowing much about them but making up names for them and telling white lies when she asked whether they had mothers and fathers.

"The papas", I said to her, "are bumblebees." Then I thought I better change the subject. She liked best the one I called a buttercup though I do not know what it really was except it was definitely not a dandelion. I rubbed her nose with one of the petals and told her now she would always be beautiful because of the curse of the buttercup; there would be nothing she could do about it, I said, for beautiful and slender she would always be. She giggled as kids will when kidded and so pretty soon I felt good and was up walking around.

Best of all was, I knew what to do about my big problem of getting a husband. The answer had come to me one morning between dawn and breakfast when all you think about is how quiet and good-smelling the world is, and what you dreamt of in the night. I wrote a certain letter. Only it was not to any ad in the paper placed there by any distinguished bachelor. A few days later the answer to it was in the box along with the reminder from the gas company.

"Melody," I said that night at dinner when Mrs. Krangsprush was sitting at the table too..."Melody, we're goin' for a long bus ride, you and your mamma."

"When?" You could tell she was tickled pink. "When we goin', Mamma?" She did not care where, either Just so it was quick. That's kids.

"Soon as we get packed up and settled here."

Mrs. Krangsprush was all ears. "Why, Irene, what in heaven's name you going to do?"

"I've got me a job at the army post upstate."

I said it in such a way that she knew my mind was made up firm. Mrs. K. was one to raise objections to any notions that did not come from herself and so she frowned for a minute not swallowing the bite of food that was on her tongue. I know now she was either a saint or out of her head but it was blessed to have her on hand for

Melody in those tough times. Still there are things a woman decides for herself and this getting a husband from somewhere was in the front of my head. The God Mrs. K. talked about would not like the idea of me, a full-bloomed lady, going to waste. A lot of good men were in the army and I figured there would be more to pick from than in the vestibule of the church on Sunday morning where they are mostly all married to start out with. And so my mind was made up.

Mrs. Krangsprush choked down that bite she had trouble getting swallowed. "Irene, that's no place for a single lady. There's dangers galore connected with living near soldiers."

But I did not think about it being any danger. It was not likely I would get scalped by any washing machine working at the PX. Two young married people from the church moved into my house paying very cheap rent so they would take good care of the place and Mrs. Bruce, the upstairs tenant, would send me her money-order each first of the month. Mrs. Krangsprush's feelings were hurt a little but she helped me with arranging for the trip.

Three weeks later I and Melody took the midnight bus out of town headed north and I felt the good feeling of knowing I had taken things in my own hands and had not bawled for a long time. I with the sloppy heart like an old grapefruit that has been bounced around ever since it fell off the tree was doing something that would lick the weepiness for ever.

The bus was crowded with mostly soldiers. Melody sat on my lap. I was hoping there would be some older fellows than these up at the post because of not wanting to feel like a mamma to the man I got married to. The driver turned the inside lights off. Melody sat still and was happy just looking out the window. The little soldier on the next seat nuzzled his face into my shoulder and slept. I let him. It was a starry night like a poem. We passed a big lake where you could see lights across the water making a reflection. Melody kept saying how everything was pretty on the bus at night-time and I was glad she had a good eye for all that beauty. If kids her age have dreams she probably dreamt that night. So did I.

The next three days were hell.

I had to be asked questions by three officers, not to speak of one civilian lady and a doctor's examination. Then it was forms to fill out. At least dozens.

And where to live.

I by accident luckily enough ran into Agnes, a soldier's wife. Her I met in the little town half a mile from the post where there was a drugstore soda fountain. I and Melody were eating lunch and Agnes was smoking while Marvin, her little boy, ate ice-cream. Agnes had brownish hair like mine but not combed even though she was pretty enough and otherwise slender, I might even say skinny. We got to talking. First about the kids. I made over her Marvin and vice versa till pretty soon the talk got around to where was I going to live.

Another hour and I had an apartment of my own in the same court just off the main street where Agnes's place was. It had a bathroom and a living-room that turned into a bedroom at night, plus on one end a place to cook food. The other ladies in the court were all married to different soldiers from the post and they had what is called a child pool where you watch all their kids one day a week and they take turns with you. My day was Sundays.

Being settled was a good feeling.

A good feeling until I turned out the lights that night to get some sleep before the big day of beginning work and then I did some weeping with the lights out because of it being a strange place and not like home and the feeling of being not connected with where I was or anything else much, a lady alone with hard work in front of her and no real grounds for hoping things would get better.

Hugo, why did you have to be such a louse? It wouldn't have killed you to get a job and do a little supporting of those who loved you, namely me and Melody. Then I would be laying in your bed asleep by this time. All right, Hugo, you go to hell even though I loved you a lot. Too much if the truth was known.

Yes, I did weep some that night, even with thinking about old Krangsprush and her positive thoughts and I wondered if positive thoughts was enough to get a soldier interested in me and Melody; sure, they'd all be wild about her but that was not the problem exactly even though it helped some. Well, here I was and there she was right next to me already asleep. Good night, Melody. I kissed her.

Now an army post has got a good number of PX's, but the one they put me behind the counter of was for the men in the hospital. I and another lady worked it alone selling all kinds of articles from candy, tobacco, jewellery, even to cameras and other souvenirs, pillow covers that either said "U.S. Army" on the top of them in embroidery or else they said "To My Mother".

The other lady was almost as skinny as Agnes and she was the frowning type that makes everything more serious than you give a darn for if you have got a sense of humour. Which I have. The men that came to me ended up by laughing before they left the counter—it was a kind of a game I played. If they was in a sour mood I worked on bringing them out of it. That way I and they had a circus between us whether it was toothpaste they were after or aspirin.

In the afternoon it was up to me to sit in a little booth in the recreation hall upstairs passing out ping-pong bats and doing what I could to help the ones that wanted to kill time. I and one of the up-patients name of Charley played Chinese checkers and generally got along like old pals, him calling me Irene by my first name right from the start.

The next afternoon Charley brought two friends of his upstairs to the rec hall and we played some pinochle. Those up-patients were a special thing, almost like a big party. No heavy eyebrows to speak of and nobody's sickness sticking out like any crucifix. There is something about getting shot up or otherwise laid low that shows a man how to laugh longer and louder than anybody else.

There was one man that laughed with everything he had except his eyes. His eyes sat still as if even while a thing was being funny, it was mostly not funny. He was a long, lanky sergeant name of R. D. Burklemaster, a mountain man from North Carolina, and the R. D. was a big secret what with nobody knowing what it stood for. Charley called him Roister Doister.

I and R. D. were partners for a few hands and did a lot of looking back and forth across the table. There wasn't anybody taking the cards serious so we barked at each other for making the wrong plays and generally speaking hit it off quite swell.

In bed that night with the lights off I thought some more about Roister Doister, wondering how the Maker ever dreamed up such an ugly face to put on top of that stack of bones. I could see him walking around in his hills where he came from, sticking out higher than any pine tree, just walking along leading with his face. I could see him all alone at the top of a mountain, laughing, even with nobody else around, and cocking his big red ear, quick so he can catch the echo. Laughing good and loud, too, except for his eyes.

At work the next morning I heard a deep voice come from up around the ceiling somewhere and I knew it was the sergeant.

"Hello, sergeant," I said to him, looking up.

"Hello, Irene," he said to me, looking down.

He bought a ten-cent package of razor blades and stood around for a minute trying to think up something to say. I made small talk about it being almost summer.

That is how things got more or less started between I and the sergeant. In the evening Melody stayed with Agnes while I met R. D. at the three-two cellar which is below the main floor of the rec hall, a place where the soldiers drink ten-cent beer that does not do much in the way of getting them drunk. I wore the dress that hides fifty pounds and put on some fresh lipstick. Judging from the flattery those fellows passed out I must have been looking not bad.

"Where's your glass?" said R. D. We were sitting at a long table, him across from me.

"No beer, thanks."

"Don't thank me, Irene. You're buying."

"I know, sergeant. That's why I'm not drinkin'."

"Strictly hard liquor, gal?"

We had a swell time and I was learning to play up to that ugly poker face.

On the next Sunday the sergeant got a pass and came over to the court where I was taking my turn looking after Melody and the other kids. He knew which one was mine without even stopping to guess. After the sun went down I opened a few cans and made what we ate look like home cooking what with a little touching up. Melody was backward at first about talking to the sergeant, she was scared of him being so tall; then there was his face, too, which you don't see the like of every day. Finally she said to me:

"Mamma, is he the tallest man in the world?"

"I guess he is, honey," I said, winking at the sergeant.

"Nope," he said, "there's one taller."

"Who?" says Melody with her eyes bugging.

"Don't know the fella's name. They got him in jail."

"What for?"

"Bent down and kissed the moon one night. The moon's husband had him run in."

Melody was still thinking about the poor old moon when I put her to bed an hour later.

"Who's the moon's husband?" she said.

"I'll ask him", I said, "and tell you in the morning."

Then I and the sergeant went for a walk.

"We *could* go to the movies tonight," he said, " 'cept for one thing ...I'm embarrassed."

"Financial?"

"Yep."

Then we went to the movies. It was Betty Hutton having quintuplets and not doing so much clowning, but it was good. He held on to my hand except during the newsreel when they showed the Korea pictures and then he just held his own knees.

After the show I could tell he had beer on his mind but what with not having any paydays as yet and the trip costing more than was sensible, I was running a little short myself. But I knew Mrs. Bruce, the upstairs tenant, would be sending her cheque along in a day or two and I could borrow it, this once, and skip a payment on the house. Alter all when a man is in the hospital on account of war and then sees the newsreels and Betty Hutton having all those babies to boot it is some little strain no doubt. We went into a noisy place where he had three beers and I some ginger ale.

He did some talking. He said he was a salesman when they did not have wars going on and made a lot of money. His sick daddy in the mountains ate up the best part of his army pay. Somebody on the enemy side of the war had shot him in the chest. He showed me the scar and said the doctor had clipped out one of his lungs.

By the time a month went by I and the sergeant got to be quite a habit. Irene, you look like a gal's in love, says the skinny lady behind the counter. Careful of that lanky one, Irene honey, says Agnes, he looks like he'd take a lady for a ride. Shut up, Agnes, says Agnes's husband, Irene knows what she's doing. You a little overboard for Roister Doister? says Charley. Where's your big sergeant, Irene? says the corporal at the gate when I go through alone one night.

I guess it showed.

There was me caught in this cyclone that usually happens to ladies slightly younger and somewhat skinnier, but liking it too much to care or think it over much. We go for a boat ride on the big lake of a summer Sunday, Melody between us, I and Roister Doister kicking the gong around like kids. You and me and Melody, says the sergeant over and over again. You and me and Melody—and the boat comes in, us tireder than hell. We sleep on the bus takes you back to the post. I wake up, the sergeant stroking my face with a couple of his long fingers like I was a puppy not weighing in at no two hundred and sixty pounds and I think all the while how he'd said on the boat ...You and me and Melody, Irene ...again and again, happier than an idiot in a sideshow and him with his ugly face sticking up half-way to the top of the bus. You could understand how he was always broker this time than the last what with the sick daddy and what-not and besides

Melody was in love with him even before I'd thought what happened to me.

It was like he was Hugo and I was a young girl. When he looked at me I felt as pretty and skinny as a statue standing in the middle of a fountain in the park somewhere with coloured lights coming off of my skin. And the more I looked at that ugly face of his the better I liked it. I even thought if it ever turned out that a certain thing happened, there might be more going on in his eyes when he laughed good and loud; that scared quiet look that made things not so funny any more might go away for good. It would be like we both got cured on account of I and him getting together.

One Sunday night we put Melody to bed tucking her in like a mamma and papa. The sergeant says I ain't going to the post tonight, Irene, and he bends over to where his lips are like a breeze crossing my face near the eyebrows and I say where you planning on sleeping, Roister Doister?

That town had its Sunday night feeling about it when we walked along toward the edge of it, except in I and the sergeant there was things going on that didn't have nothing to do with Sunday or any other day. I had a feeling like you're riding along in a Carnival Bug, the ride that whips you around corners in and out so fast you're about ten feet ahead of your stomach and when the Bug stops you wait for your stomach to catch up. I had that feeling as we walked along and I liked it, but not knowing what would come of it I worried some, and here's the sergeant's tremendous arm reaching all the way around me at the shoulders and here's my arm hanging on to him at the waist, us walking along like we knew where we was going even though the subject had not been brought up and when we got there I wept.

He says, "The man at the desk thought we were married to each other, Irene."

But that did not stop me weeping, nothing could. Good Christ, you'd wonder where all that salt water comes in from in the first place and I sat there on the edge of the bed knowing it must be piped in from the ocean or some place wishing to hell I could dry up and behave. He lights a cigarette and sits on the bed three feet from me and I think about how being together with somebody is more right than being alone three feet away with a whole war sewed up underneath your scars.

I stopped weeping.

After he turned out the light what happened was a sin but I don't say he's to blame any more than me and whatever it is in the world we try to get from it.

Before dawn the man knocked on the door and said five o'clock, folks, like we'd asked him to do. The sergeant had to be at the post at six and I wanted to get home before Melody woke up. He got out of bed right away without saying a word or touching me and got himself dressed. I was scared. He was not Hugo and he was not hardly even Roister Doister. It was like waking up with a stranger in the same bed and I wondered why he would not even look at me or say good morning to make things easier.

"Good morning, Burk," I said to him.

"Irene, you got some money?"

"In my purse. Get it."

"I got to give him four more dollars."

"Who?"

"The clerk."

He took five dollars from my purse and started for the door.

"What's wrong, Burk?"

"I'll wait for you downstairs." And then he left.

I did not dare start to think or to weep for there would be no shutting it off. I pressed my teeth together and got dressed good and fast and left the room, glad to get that door shut behind me.

He was standing on the sidewalk, leaning against the hotel doorway smoking himself a cigarette. Out of the corner of his eye he could see I was there but he would not look at me. We walked back into the centre of town while the sun was coming up and it was more than a mile before he opened his mouth. I will not say what I felt like I was.

"Irene," he says finally, his eyes straight in front of him, "you're a good woman, but I have not done the right thing by you."

"Who says you haven't?"

"I mean like you having to give me the money to pay up the room. That ain't right."

"Don't think about that, Burk," I said to him.

He was just ashamed because of the money, I thought, and it was a relief to believe he was not ashamed of something else. We walked along for another while, him with his eyes about a mile higher than the street.

"Maybe we ought to get married, Irene."

"Maybe so," I said.

"Suppose we better wait till I get outa the army?"

"That's up to you, Burk."

"Then we'd have some money to do it up with."

"You like a big wedding?" I asked him.

"No, but I thought you..."

"Not me," I said.

"You want to do the thing right away, Irene?"

"Whatever you say, Burk."

I kissed Melody on the cheek lightly so as not to wake her up.

Then there was a mirror in front of me and the face looking through it was pretty as anything you see in technicolour and inside of me the sound track would not quit.

How do you do, Mrs. R. D. Burklemaster-to-be, Mrs. Roister Doister from North Carolina. Maybe it is a mountain wife which I will become, carrying wood, drawing water from a well, wringing honey out of a hive of bees, watching Melody grow up in the pine-tree sunshine with a man bigger than Abraham Lincoln watching over I and her; or maybe it is a city lady I will remain or maybe we will live in a tent pitched on an iceberg somewhere in the middle of an ocean. Did that make any difference? No, not one hell of a least little bit of a difference.

A week later we had our plans made. R. D. applied for a furlough of fourteen days and they gave it to him. I gave my notice at the PX and phoned home to the lady living in my house downstate. She got the extra rooms ready upstairs and expected the bride and groom a week from Sunday morning. Roister Doister wanted a secret wedding so as to avoid the heckling from all his soldier-boy buddies.

That was all right.

I did not care.

So it was to be a secret wedding in the living-room of the preacher. Four o'clock. Saturday afternoon. R. D. was embarrassed to borrow the eighty-four dollars from me which I had held out once again from the payment on the house. He kept saying maybe we ought to wait till he could pay for the thing himself and do it up, but I told him, no, Burklemaster, this is a joint thing, we can wait for something else, perhaps, but not for eighty-four dollars; I made him see light and finally he took it without being ashamed.

On the Friday night, the night before the wedding, Roister Doister kissed me hard. He looked at me in the eyes and he wrapped his big arms around me and said in a shaking kind of a voice that was filled with loving me: You are a good woman, Irene,

And I wept.

He went through the gate and I stood weeping, not even seeing clear any more through all the being happy that watered down my face. Good-bye until tomorrow, my heart said to him. I watched him like through a rainy windshield as he walked away with his head high as an office building.

Roister Doister.

Jesus, he was a tall good man. And mine.

The corporal at the gate stepped out of his box when he saw me standing there alone.

"You all right, Irene?" he said, knowing good and well I was weeping.

"You bet your shirt I'm all right, Corporal!" I said, jabbing him in the stomach with my fist, but not hard. Then I walked away.

"G'night, Irene," he said.

Overhead was a deep, sea-blue sky.

" 'Night, Corporal."

Melody was bewildered. The idea of a daddy would not sink in. But she would sooner or later get the idea.

I packed our things and got them to the bus station in a taxicab. Agnes had to know the secret on account of she had to take care of Melody while I and the sergeant was busy doing the thing at the preacher's house. Agnes kissed me and wished me luck and sprayed me with French perfume. At three-thirty I went off to meet R. D. in the lobby of the big hotel.

I knew walking along the street that I would remember every touch of the day. I'd lost a hundred pounds just thinking about it and was walking on balls of cotton instead of a sidewalk and everything I passed reached out and kissed me. That boom-town thrown together out of sticks during the war got to be home suddenly and all the people smiled back at me as though I'd known them all my life instead of not at all. You'd have thought they knew the secret and was wishing me well for the rest of my life.

I knew I would remember how it felt to be so happy.

And I knew I would remember the hotel lobby and how empty it was when I got there and the clerk when he asked me was I waiting for one of the guests and the pitch of my voice when I said Thank you, sir, no I am being married this afternoon and am waiting here for my husband-to-be. And the clerk's deep good smile hot with his deep good wishes. And the air going out of my heart gradually as the hand of the big clock moved past four o'clock, and how the hundred pounds I had lost getting dressed came back to me as it moved past five and the way the belief in miracles froze inside of my head when I called the preacher at five-thirty and said, sir, there has been an accident; I and the sergeant will be late, sir, I am very sorry.

Yes. Late.

At six o'clock I did not weep. And I did not weep at seven.

At eight o'clock I went to the phone and called the corporal at the gate.

"Corporal," I said, "this is Irene. I am the lady friend of the big sergeant."

"H'lo, Irene."

"Corporal," I said, "have you seen that big ugly bastard?"

"Sure, honey," said the corporal. "He got hisself discharged this morning and took off on an aeroplane."

"Is that a fact, Corporal? I wonder where he took off to."

"Asheville, North Carolina, honey."

"Thank you very kindly, Corporal."

"Everything okay, Irene?"

"You bet your shirt everything is okay." That's what I remember saying to the corporal, that he could bet his shirt everything was okay.

I and Melody took the eleven-o-two out of town headed south, downstate, headed for home. The bus was crowded. She just sat on my lap but I could not feel her being there. I just looked at her till she went to sleep. Nothing was going on much in my head for the first hundred miles of the way home. I just looked at Melody and had thoughts about being a kid and not a woman, about how kids look forward all their years to being grown-ups and about what they get when they are.

About what kids get when they are grown-ups. About how it does not help to have something soft and rotten as a grapefruit for a heart. It's a mother's job to put something firm in there, about the texture of a rock. Sensitive kids get it hard; they live to be old men and ladies and they bawl along through life in pain up till the time they die. They like to look at lights across the water and to have buttercups smashed into their noses and to be told the world is cream on top of sweet peaches. But you got to knock that out of them.

You got to or somebody says shut-up at the right time, a real whammy comes along, a pet goldfish dies in the bowl, or somebody forgets to smile and right away the grapefruit heart begins to stink and squirt juicy tears out of their eyes.

Melody woke up. She looked out of the window.

"It's pretty on the bus at night-time," she said. I slapped her good. She cried. "Go to sleep," I said. She cried some more. I hugged her. It is a job to teach them, to give them the right kind of heart, to dry them up young.

I have not wept, not once since that day, and I looked up some of my old clients and they let me come back to clean their offices again, and Mrs. Krangsprush talks about positive thoughts and sometimes I wonder what you can buy how much of for eighty-four dollars.

Miguel

Christmas morning Miguel awakened in a room he had never seen before; the city itself might have been Chicago, it might have been St. Louis. Wherever he was, he was not in Montevideo.

Dear Mamacita, he had written to her in Spanish on Thanksgiving Day, Dear Mamacita, I love you and miss you very much and it may be at Christmas-time they will give me a vacation and I am saving my money for the aeroplane. The letter you wrote me was a beautiful letter, Mamacita. Yes, I wear the medal of St. Christopher at my throat. Please give my love to Paolo, Diego, Maria, and kiss Pappa and Grandma. It may be at Christmas-time...

In the middle of the year Miguel, at eighteen, had sailed on a tramp steamer to New Orleans and after he had been there a few weeks he knew he would never again live with his family in Uruguay. Dear Mamacita, he wrote to her then: I have a job with an American company, they are taking me to San Francisco where I will teach dancing in a big school. I love you and I will be home for Christmas.

The man who took Miguel to San Francisco was the customer's man for a brokerage house whom he had met in the French Quarter. There was no dancing school. They drove up and across the United States in a large automobile and moved into a suite in a Nob Hill hotel.

When they had been settled in that city for two weeks, Miguel felt he knew his way around. One night when his friend, whose name was Eric, returned to the hotel, Miguel pretended to be asleep. He watched the man place a large stack of money under the paper in the dresser drawer. When he got into bed Miguel continued to watch carefully and after a while the broker was asleep. Then Miguel dressed very quietly, took the money and went away.

The next day he was sorry for what he had done. Eric had been kind to him; when he looked at Miguel his brown eyes had been filled with trust and flecked with gold, and now Miguel hated himself for the betrayal.

But he did not hate himself for long. He counted the money and knew that he would not have to work for a long time. He found a room in a small hotel on the cheaper side of Nob Hill.

Now, all alone, he smoked a cigarette and looked into the mirror that hung on the wall. Miguel's teeth were very white; he flashed them at the reflection in the glass. His eyes were very large, outlined with black lashes; he winked them at his mirror eyes: Hello Miguel, he said to himself, and then he smiled and blew a cloud of smoke at himself.

Dear Mamacita, San Francisco is a beatiful city, but not so beautiful as Montevideo. I love you, Mamacita, but please do not ask me to come home yet. I am beginning to learn to make my way...

In the evening Miguel dressed in his new suit, a white one, and a dark green tie over a salmon pink shirt. He started out to enjoy the city alone.

San Francisco is largely a matter of bridges, hills, people and water; and cable cars.

The cable cars are like this: underneath the streets you hear a certain clattering whirr from some subterranean beast whose job it is to push and pull the toy-like trolleys up and down the hills of San Francisco. The long-time dwellers of this city seem to take the cable cars for granted but for Miguel they are a sad and merry ride through a circus of romance. As part of this cargo of flesh and hearts, you cling to the vertical bar and begin the steep climb; far ahead of you at the horizon, at the top of the city, another identical cluster of living begins its descent; within a few moments it is possible to distinguish one being from the others coming toward you; it is dressed in yellow, it carries an umbrella, it is slender, it is a woman; a block closer and you know the woman is young, her hair is brown, she is pretty and her dark eyes are wide open and clinging to yours. Now there is that briefest of all moments when the two cable cars pass midway up the hill, and stop only a few inches apart. Her desire, pure as a white angel towering over a Christmas tree, reaches into the space between you where your eyes meet. Unpleading, uncompromising, there is a moment of interlocking thought: I could love such a one as you, as you, love you I love you, and the impulse to leap on to the descending car is strongest now, such a one as you, I love you I love you; but one does not leap, and the cable car, lurching and tugging and grinding, draws the image out of focus; one continues to follow with one's eyes: I could have loved you; it is a woman, it is slender, it carries an umbrella, it is dressed in yellow; and now it is a faraway cable car. One has not leapt and one is sad. What is wrong with a world in which one does not leap across the infinitesimal gap of time and space which separates him from his love?

But the heart of Miguel is a chameleon and it stretches itself lizard-like in new and rainbow places, retreating with the first cloud and reappearing under the next sun. Down Market Street, up Flower to Nob Hill all the way to the top, down again, over California, in and out of the avenues some of which were lined with shops and others with antique apartment buildings of grey and red and brown. Miguel saw one grey apartment building with golden doors and through a third-storey window he saw a certain lighted interior whose colours were heavier than blood. A blond tall man emerged from the building and as Miguel continued down the street, his pace somewhat slackened, he could sense in the air a dark and private sun waiting to shine on his lizard heart. Miguel turned around, allowed his eyes to linger for a moment and then, somewhat self-consciously, he continued his walk. At the next corner, waiting for the traffic light to turn green, the man stood at his side. Hello.

Hello. I am Miguel.

Miguel and his new friend went to a secret place. There was a sign on the door which said: For Members Only. Up two flights of stairs, through a corridor and beyond an archway, there was a large bar-room filled with men of all types and sizes. A blind Negro woman played the piano, the drummer was a white man in a yellow satin shirt— mostly he used a cymbal and a pair of rhumba gourds— and one fat colourless face poured air into a horn. Everyone turned to view the arrivals and the gathering was altogether dazzled by the figure of Miguel in his new white suit, dark green tie, and salmon pink shirt. His new friend, whose name was Edward, bought the drinks. Miguel chose rum. Glass in hand, he wandered to the platform where the music was being made. Many eyes followed. Within an hour a fat man had bought Miguel a drink; so had a bald-headed man, a tall man with an acne-cracked face, and a thin little wizened-up professor-looking creature. To each of them he gave his name and a smile and wandered away. Then he began to dance and everyone applauded the young Latin in the white suit who performed a real South American rhumba. Then the wizened-up professor-looking creature bought him another drink, the man with the acne-cracked face turned away with disdain, the bald man and the fat man grinned, and then there was a drink from someone else, and soon he had wandered back to his new friend, whose name was Edward. Edward said Would you like to go home with me Miguel, and Miguel was feeling very happy.

The next morning Edward was up and dressed and had left the apartment before Miguel had awakened. The walls of the bedroom were green-almost-black and the woodwork was white. On the bedstand was a note: Miguel, I am at the office, call me when you wake up. I put some money in your pocket for cab fare. But don't forget to call me. Edward.

Miguel could not remember Edward's face, but in his pocket was a twenty-dollar bill. Miguel dressed and boarded first a cable car, then a bus, and soon he was in his little hotel room.

Dear Mamacita, the Americans like my dancing and they learn very quickly. Please do not worry about me for I may become very rich if I work hard. Besides I love you and miss you...

Then Miguel sat talking to his flashing white teeth and big black eyes in the mirror: They like you here in San Francisco, Miguel. The Americans will always like you and give you money and you will give them your smile and your rhumba; you will save your money for Christmas-time and every day write a penny post card to Mamacita and tell her that you love her.

For several days Miguel explored the city and for several nights he explored the bar-rooms.

One day he boarded a bus which carried him across the Golden Gate Bridge into Marin County. It was September and the sun was shining and the wind was blowing. He walked along the boardwalk which stretched along the bay. There were small pleasure boats moored to the docks and farther out there were larger boats, barges, schooners and houseboats, fishing boats and sail boats. Long-haired women wearing slacks and sweaters and men in tattered trousers and sweatshirts were everywhere, in and out of the boats, on the docks, along the boardwalks.

Miguel was sitting crosslegged on the boardwalk eating a pear when a young man stopped to talk with him. He was a thin man with a large-boned face and his head was covered with small tight curls. He wore white ducks, a torn blue shirt, and was barefooted.

When they had talked for a few minutes Miguel and the stranger, whose name was Carl, walked along the boardwalk together, and climbed into a small made-over fishing boat where the young man lived. There were the strong smells of a deeper sea clinging to the old wooden boards and there were the fainter smells of long-dead fish; inside the cabin, however, there were only the smells of paintings, the strong sweet effluvium of linseed oil that Miguel could never forget. The walls of the cabin were stacked six and seven deep with large door-size canvases on which had been painted sombre-coloured tales of suffering. On one was a leaf-green Jesus Crucified, and Miguel made the Sign of the Cross; on another was a dead child with a blue face in the arms of a weeping mourning madonna, and Miguel thought of Mamacita.

Carl poured water into a pan of old coffee-grounds, lighted a fire under it, and sat down. Miguel looked at Carl, Carl looked at Miguel. They smoked. The coffee began to boil and the smell of it was added to the rich air of the bay.

Carl drew pencil sketches of Miguel and in the later afternoon he outlined in charcoal a large door-size canvas. They ate dinner together and in the later evening they drank wine together.

In the morning Carl swept the deck of the made-over fishing boat on which he lived, and Miguel, inside, watched him through the cabin window. In the air was the smell of long-dead fishes, and a deeper sea, there was linseed oil in the air and a crackling moist morning smell, and on the small burner the coffee-grounds boiled once again. Altogether there was in the air an invitation to breathe. Miguel left the cabin, stood on the dock, he looked down at Carl who had stopped sweeping to look at his new friend.

Miguel boarded a bus which carried him across the Golden Gate to San Francisco. He went to the little hotel room, put his clothing and toilet articles into a suitcase, looked into the mirror but did not wink at himself, did not wink at the new sad softer vision of himself; his eyes did blink once, though, for they were covered with a strange warm moist film of tears, and the pupils were flecked with gold.

Dear Mamacita, he wrote to her in Spanish, last night I met a girl at the dancing school and we went for a boat ride. She is a Catholic girl with brown eyes. I love you very much, and please kiss Pappa and Grandmamma and...

When Miguel stepped off the bus, he saw Carl watching him from the end of the boardwalk; each of their faces was open in a wide white smile. Carl turned and began to walk the long mile back to his boat, Miguel followed several yards behind. The wind was blowing, they walked slowly, in procession through the afternoon, past the docks on which were moored pleasure boats and larger boats, fishing boats and sail boats. The women with long hair and the men in sweatshirts smiled and waved to Carl and Carl raised his arm and tossed back his head, greeting them, as the two young men walked the long mile.

Miguel was happy and for many days he did not write a penny post card to his mother. Carl gave him a pair of tattered trousers, a sweatshirt, a sailor's cap, and together they scraped and chipped away the old dead paint from the fishing boat on which Carl and Miguel now lived. They did not talk much; Carl's language was a mid-European one and Miguel's was Spanish. But one afternoon Carl stopped his work and said to Miguel: "A man who does not work well, does not love well."

Miguel worked hard on the boat, alone much of the time, while Carl applied colour to the large door-size canvas for which his Latin friend had posed. Miguel was sorry he had taken money from some of the Americans without having earned it; he scraped and chipped away the old dead paint until the boards were bare. He learned to work hard.

After many days of travelling landlocked across the ocean of this labour, after covering the bare boards of the fishing boat with a green deeper than any sea—Miguel painted a pair of black and white eyes on the bow of the boat, just as he had seen in photographs of certain Italian fishing craft: Day and night, we see where we are going, said the eyes of the boat on which Carl and Miguel now lived. Carl laughed when he saw the eyes.

"Miguel," he said, "I have finish the painting."

He brewed some coffee, using fresh beans in the pot. They smoked. Miguel looked at the painting. Here was Christ, his Resurrection, a pure white Jesus, ascending into Heaven, and the face of Christ was Miguel's. Miguel made the Sign of the Cross. Carl laughed. They smoked and in the later afternoon they ate dinner. In the evening Carl and Miguel walked far out along the ridge overlooking Marin County, and on their left was the sea. Miguel prayed. In the later evening they drank red wine in the fishing boat which was clean now, painted with the labour of Miguel, painted a deeper sea-green than any depth of ocean; they drank wine in the fishing boat whose eyes were black and white and seeing, more seeing than human eyes.

While they slept the famous fog came out of hiding.

The famous fog, like a black bold monster squatting on a dream, descended upon the bay.

Miguel awakened with a sneeze. It was morning. The coffee was brewing. Carl was dressed and working.

He had begun a new canvas, a larger wall-size canvas.

Miguel's suitcase stood in the doorway of the cabin. They drank the coffee in silence. They smoked. Carl nodded, indicating the suitcase.

"The painting is finish," he said.

There is no sun in any heaven strong enough to penetrate the fog of San Francisco Bay. Carl tied a thick woollen scarf about his throat, Miguel buttoned the collar of his shirt, turned his coat collar up at the neck. Carl carried the bag across the boardwalk, Miguel followed several yards behind. No wind blew for the fog had eaten the world. They walked rapidly as the earth stood still, they walked rapidly on the march through the black morning, past the docks where fishing boats and sail boats were moored side by side with pleasure boats and larger boats, along the bay where the visit of the sun had been forgotten. It was like walking through some lifeless valley of the moon and in the air was an invitation to die.

The bus pushed through the fog, rolled into the golden arms of the bridge. The great extended arms of the golden bridge brought the bus into the body of the city; and the cold concrete womb opened mechanically, sunless, warming no one.

Dear Mamacita, he wrote her from the bus station. The Catholic girl with brown eyes is dead. There was an accident on the cable car and she was killed. The American company is sending me to Los Angeles where the cinema stars live. Mamacita, I miss you, and I love you. Please wait until Christmas-time. Kiss Paolo and Maria and Grandmamma...

But Christmas morning Miguel awakened in a room he had never seen before and the city might have been Chicago or St. Louis; wherever he was, he was not in Montevideo. For there was snow on the windowsill and a Christmas sun burned through the glass.

Laughter in the Graveyard

I certainly didn't know who he thought he was, sitting there on Kurkowski's front porch with his legs crossed, his feet resting on the knee-high wooden railing, a long cigarette dangling from his lips. In the first place he didn't look old enough to smoke without catching hell for it and in the second place I instinctively disliked him because he looked like I wanted to look myself: handsome and dark, tall and slender, about seventeen, and his features just perfect enough to make anybody hate his guts on sight. He wore wine-coloured slacks and a dark green sweater, royal colours, and now as I remember him my mind paints turrets on the roof of his house and a crown of gold on top of his head.

It was the last warm day of the year I was fourteen and all about the earth and the houses and the streets was an amber late September glow. I'd just returned from school and there he was—the Kurkowskis lived across the street from us in a house just like ours, five-room frame, porch across the front, bushes on the lawn—there he was, seated in a canvas chair with this colossal cigarette sticking out of him.

I went to the kitchen. Mother was peeling potatoes for dinner. I kissed her.

"Who's 'at guy on Kurkowski's porch?" I said.

"His name is Steve."

"He the one that's bin in Canada, at some school?"

"That's right, David," she said, "only now he's come home to live, he's going to live at home now with Dolores and his papa."

Dolores was Kurkowski's oldest daughter. It was Mother's theory that even though she was pretty and had fine, naturally curly black hair, Dolores was too fat ever to find a husband; that's why she stayed home and kept house for her father. Mrs. Kurkowski had been dead for ten years and Steve had been sent to a boarding school in Ontario. Mr. Kurkowski owned a beer garden and a dry goods store and he had more money than anyone else's father, at least on our street.

"Honest? I mean how do *you* know, Mother? Maybe he's just visiting on a vacation or something."

"Dolores was here this afternoon. She told me Steve's a very sick boy."

"Sick?"

Mother rinsed off a potato and dropped it into the pan of water.

"It's his heart. They call it enlarged. His poor heart just keeps growing and growing and one of these day's it'll puff out to where it touches his ribs."

"How come it grows so much?"

"It just does, there's something wrong with it. We don't know about these things, David; it's medical. But when his heart gets too big and touches his bones, then Steve's going to be dead."

"Dead!"

No wonder they let him smoke! He *was* somebody special. I started out the door to have another look at him.

"David! David Gillady, come back here."

Mother turned the faucet and the water stopped. She turned to look at me.

"David, I wouldn't go run telling all my friends about this. Now after all, it's bad enough. How would you feel, everybody knowing and looking at you?"

"Yeah."

Then I went to the front porch so that I could look across at Steve. He'd put out his cigarette and sat perfectly still with his hands folded across his stomach, leaning back, his eyes dreaming high into the locust tree in our front yard. It seemed funny the way you could go from hating someone to really liking him, all in ten minutes flat, just because you had a piece of information. And Steve, with all his quiet and early repose in the face of that impending doom seemed suddenly older and wise. He knew just what to do: sit on the porch of a five-room house in Cleveland, smoke a cigarette, wait for it, look into a tree.

I wondered what on earth could be seen in a tree by the dying; the wings of an angel coming at you, God's heart, open and red and warm like a bed you crawl back into, all those secrets of death and hell? Or just leaves, red yellow crumbling falling dying, like yourself.

Mr. Kurkowski's car pulled up in the driveway and Steve's father got out carrying a huge package. He was smiling and mumbling tunelessly in Polish the words of some folk song. Then he spoke to Steve.

"Hello, Pop," said Steve and he glanced superiorly at the old man as if he were vaguely amused in some bitter way with his father's good humour, and turned away. The package was of great bulk and seemed to be heavy. Mr. Kurkowski carried it up the steps, placed it on the porch floor, and with care and probably pain, he stood straight, stretching his back, grunting from the effort.

He walked over to Steve and placed his arm around his son's shoulders, but Steve didn't seem to care one way or another for the old man's affection. I couldn't hear what was said but after a moment Mr. Kurkowski opened the package. It contained an electric phonograph. Steve's interest was instantly aroused. He stood up, walked over to the machine, touched it with his fingers as if it were a dog or something living, and began to smile.

By now the old man was so happy he laughed out loud. He carried the phonograph into the house and Steve followed him. A few minutes later the music of jazz leaked from every seam of the house and poured from all the open windows.

Dolores visited Mother every day and they drank coffee together and smoked cigarettes. The talk was always of Steve. Sometimes Dolores would cry when she spoke of him and his impending death. She and the rest of the Kurkowskis, Edwin and his wife, Bernadine and her husband, the children and all the aunts and uncles, plotted like conspirators to make Steve happy, looked constantly for new ways to delight him. They gave him the use of their cars and often when Steve was not sitting on his front porch dreaming into the locust tree, he would be getting into a car alone or with some of his relatives and they would go off to the lake for a week-end of fun or to one or the other of the relatives' houses for a party.

One Saturday night there was a big party at Kurkowski's house. All day long there was the commotion of supplies arriving, beer and Coca Cola being loaded into the basement, and at sunset the caterers arrived in white coats. Mother put on her black dress and high-heeled shoes, her rhinestone ear-rings and her lipstick; at nine o'clock she and Dad crossed the street. At dinner-time there'd been some glimmering of hope that I might go too, but Dad put an end to that notion by reminding me I was only fourteen. I said I'd be having a birthday in a month, but he said birthdays didn't cut any ice.

From my bedroom window I watched the people parking their cars and the house filling up and the noise getting noisier, and by midnight I was hidden crosslegged under an evergreen tree on Kurkowski's lawn. By then things were going strong. Bad-boy Billings, an ex-boxer who was now my father's drinking partner, came out at I a.m. to puke over the porch railing. His wife, who was bigger than he was, heavier, and according to my father, a better boxer, led him home on her arm. I knew if Bad-boy was drunk that meant Dad was no longer in good shape, so I returned to my bedroom window.

I could hear the phonograph playing its jazz and a hundred laughing voices, and as I fell asleep some time later I remember the wooden pillars that supported their front porch roof had begun to wiggle in rhythm, the chimney danced and the shingles fluttered to a wild boogie beat; it was as if Steve, his bad heart and the new phonograph had transformed Kurkowski's home into a carnival funhouse in which a thousand magic mirrors reflected and multiplied the faces of love and caused the laughter and jazz to resound as if the turrets I had imagined were real and the palace housed a prince.

Mother said Steve was lonely and that I should visit him. She suggested this one afternoon when I was sitting on the porch watching him. I did a lot of watching Steve in those days and a lot of thinking up ways to attract his attention. I combed my hair and shined my shoes and one day even lit up a cigar and sat on the porch smoking it. But nothing seemed to help.

One thing I never thought of was just to go ahead over and say I'm David Gillady, glad to know you. When Mother suggested this I was certain she'd lost her mind.

"Just up and visit him, he's lonely for Heaven's sake, and no one to talk to much of the time, so just go ahead."

The next time Mother talked with Dolores they must have arranged what would happen next. For one afternoon Dolores appeared on her front porch and called across to me. "David, oh David, come here a minute, honey; there's something I want you to do for me." And then I went across the street for my first close-up look at Steve.

His dark hair was carefully combed and small waves like black chicken feathers clung to his neck and the sides of his face near his ears, and here and there pointing in all directions were stubborn fragments that even his hair oil which smelled very special and must have cost at least a dollar a bottle, could not cow down into place.

One look at his clothes, the soft fine quality and the darkness of their colours, his richly tanned Slavic skin and brown gem eyes that bled amber lights, and the secret and liquid quality of his glance, at once warm and austere; the deliberate dignity with which he sat on that canvas porch chair flicking ashes into the smoking stand; one moment's exposure to his aura of death and the unspoken knowledge of mysteries seldom contemplated by one so young—and I knew that more than anything else on earth or in Heaven I wanted one thing.

To be him. To be Steve. To have presents and parties and borrowed cars, and others looking on, longing for my secret.

We became friends. He liked to talk and I liked to listen. The arrogance I had suspected was not there. He was kind and lonely. He told me in the course of many visits about the wild life he'd led away from home, about all the whorehouses and beer gardens he'd been to and the women he'd known. He wanted me to know his life had been a full one, rich with excitements; he even said the reason his heart was bad now was that he had lived too fast.

One afternoon, just ten minutes after Steve had told me the story of the girl he'd gotten in trouble in Chicago, Dolores came into the room and accidentally let out the fact that Steve hadn't ever been west of Cleveland. But I just sat there with my mouth half open and my eyes bugging out; when somebody's lying to you it makes him feel more at ease somehow to think you're pretty dumb.

He seemed to feel he was letting the world down by dying young and he lied to me to relieve himself of the guilt. For me alone he was writing a fascinating memoir composed of dreams and truth and because I believed him he became more fluent, the wishes and dreams took on the appearance of fact.

After many weeks when he had filled his seventeen years brimful with excitements and because winter had come and the snow too, we had to move our meetings from the porch to Kurkowski's living-room—Steve continued still. I knew he was extending his autobiography to include the years in which he would no longer be alive and now, instead of disappearing as words do, the scenes he invented seemed to hang in the air between us like a puppet show enacted by ghosts.

In the spring he seemed to be weary of lying and the sessions grew shorter. We would listen instead to the jazz on the phonograph or the radio. Steve liked most the music he called noncommercial jazz; he had a stack of records and many albums of early New Orleans recordings and when he talked now, it was of the jazz musicians he'd read about in books.

One evening we were listening to Louie Armstrong on the phonograph and I saw something new in Steve's eyes, a quality of inhumanly perfect remoteness, as empty of thought at that moment as gouged-out statue eyes. It was as if he had gone to meet the music somewhere outside of his body, as if in some undesignated area of the room his heart cavorted with angels, and listened to some clangorous unearthly secrets.

At the precise moment that the needle reached the inside of the disc and its scratching came through the soundbox, Steve began to laugh. He laughed until whatever had happened to him came to an end, and that took quite a while, long enough for me to become frightened. Then he asked me if I had ever read the Bible, one particular book of it which contained the prophecy of the end of the world, about how Gabriel would blow his horn and the world would come to an end. Steve told me the horn the Bible spoke of was the horn of the jazz musician and pretty soon, in a few years at the most, all the jazz musicians would be blowing their Gabriel horns, wooing God, then His sky would open up and swallow the earth and all the people and there would be no more of living for us—nothing but Heaven which was an eternal jazz song in which all the people partook.

Instead of going straight home that evening, I walked several blocks to the public school on Euclid Avenue where there was a lawn, the biggest patch of grass you could find in our area of Cleveland, The snow was melted and the earth was dry enough that you could do some lying down and looking up at the sky, a fine pastime in any decent weather, and that's what I did for maybe an hour or two while hundreds of horn-honking cars rolled by on the streets like noisy lightning bugs; two cats fought as they made love in the bushes under a schoolroom window; early spring insects buzzed a street lamp like crazy Indians dancing for rain. It was hard to imagine there being no more living on this earth, until some black heavy clouds moved in from nowhere, soggy-looking clouds that got in the way of the stars.

Then I went home.

In the morning when Mother awakened me for school she told me Dolores had phoned in the middle of the night to say that Steve had got up to go to the toilet about 4 a.m. and died on the bathroom floor.

My father was a strange man. Turnips used to give him a rash. He'd put salve on the rash and go on eating turnips. He was the same way in his treatment of me.

For instance he said I imitated Steve Kurkowski. He'd holler and cuss me out about having princely ways that he wanted to knock out of me—but it didn't matter what my ways were, he'd have knocked them out of me anyway. He was that kind of a man, the kind that likes to knock things out of people.

At seven-thirty on the morning Steve died I was sitting on the windowsill of my bedroom, just looking out doing some daydreaming into the locust tree when my father sneaked up behind me and slapped me across the back of the neck with a wet shaving towel.

"Where's your socks?" he said. When he was angry my father talked so loud you'd have thought he was a politician campaigning to be the neighbourhood heel.

"I don't know, I don't *know* where they are."

"Find 'em and get 'em on. It's late. What you sitting there about? You ought to be down in the bathroom now." He was a bug on bathrooms. "Just don't come around brushin' your teeth in the bathtub when I'm tryin' to shave."

There was nothing like his voice to knock a decent and sad thought of death out of your head. And what was I thinking about? How good it would be to cry and feel bad about poor Steve not getting to do any more living, no more wild parties and Canadian whores and phonograph records, no more nothing, not even lies because where he was going it all had to be true.

But nothing seemed sad enough so I could get some tears out. There it was, the locust tree, right between Kurkowski's house and me; and my focus changed from one to the other, to the house where Steve was dead and getting colder and colder, to the locust tree, that secret he always looked at when the leaves were falling from the branches...

"Just keep outa my way," said my father. "I don't care if you get to school late and that damn old battle-axe starts writing me notes to come and see her. Just keep outa my way, and don't come brushin' your teeth in the bathtub when I'm tryin' to shave."

Then he went away. I pulled into my socks and went on with thinking about sadness; there was a poem I'd heard in a movie once and I thought it might help me to feel bad. After all, when your friends die you're supposed to cry.

> *When I am dead my dearest,*
> *Sing no sad songs for me...*

But I couldn't remember the rest of it.

> *Just keep outa my way.*

All day long people talked of Steve. Telephone rang, cars stopped in front of his house; people came and went chattering about his sweetness, his good looks, his youth and the early ending to his life.

After dinner Mr. Kurkowski was in our living-room. He asked my father if I might be a pallbearer at the funeral and sit with Steve's body on the night before he was buried. His English was poor but you didn't have to understand the words to know he'd loved his son very much. When I entered the room Mr. Kurkowski placed his arm about my shoulder and his eyes were wet. Dad was embarrassed. He looked at Mother and started to fidget and frown. The idea of an old man weeping made him nervous.

On the second morning I saw the hearse from the funeral parlour stop in front of Kurkowski's house and two big men carried the coffin into the living-room. That morning, as if the sun were travelling backwards, the air was colder, there was a coating of white frost on the greening lawns and trees, and the earth had returned to winter. A florist's truck stopped at the curb and large funeral wreaths with frozen-looking blossoms and bouquets with flower buds that would never open were carried into the house. Then the priest arrived.

That evening, in preparation for the following night when I would spend the night sitting with Steve, Mother pressed my suit, an ill-fitting greenish tweed handed down from a cousin in Portsmouth, Ohio, who was long since dead; and I set about applying polish to a pair of shoes I'd worn three straight winters without galoshes. In each sole was a large hole and the leather was torn at the heel where my foot had worn away the threads. I left the shoes in the dining-room and went to bed. Mother came in to make the nightly adjustments: close one window, open another, fuss with the blankets, all the fiddling about mothers do to make you think you are more comfortable.

"Hey, Mother, d'you think Dolores'd let me wear Steve's wine-coloured slacks to his funeral?"

"Now, David, shame on you," she said, "you can't go to a funeral in the clothes of the person that's dead. I'd be ashamed, and Steve your best friend, you'd think you'd have better sense, good God! Don't you feel bad he's dead, David? Thinking about nothing but wine-coloured slacks?"

"Mother, is there something wrong with somebody that when somebody close dies, then that person doesn't cry or anything, or feel bad?"

"Talk sense, David, what're you asking? I can't figure out what you're asking, now say what you mean won't you? You don't feel bad Steve's dead, your best friend?"

"Of course I do, I think it's awful. He wasn't very old and it's a shame; he was a swell guy and awful young just to die like that. Only how come I don't cry, Macushlah?" That was a name I had for her when things got embarrassing and I wanted her to think I was only half-serious. She sat on the edge of the bed and placed her hand, cool and smooth, on my forehead.

"Sooner or later you'll cry, David. Lord knows he was a good boy and went straight to Heaven, but sometimes when you lose someone close, your best friend like this, you don't feel it much till long after they're in the ground. Just don't think about it, say your prayers and forget about all those wine-coloured slacks. Good night, sweetheart." And she kissed me. "Don't worry now, you'll cry sooner or later."

"Where's Dad?"

"He's out having a drink with Bad-boy. You go to sleep."

I wondered how she knew Steve went straight to Heaven. For all she knew he might have died before he got to confession in time to tell about some of his lies and was being held up in Purgatory. Just after sleep came, I was awakened by my father's voice. He'd found my shoes in the dining-room and was shouting to Mother.

"Look at these goddamn shoes. Look, Laurie, look what Bert Gillady's son's wearin' to his best friend's wake. And funeral to boot! Does he think I'm made of money? Why can't David take care of his clothes I work all week to buy? He's too damn lazy is the truth, too damn lazy to untie the strings 'fore he puts 'em on, is the truth. And they tear. Look! See? Ruined. Does he think I'm made of money, Laurie? What must I do? Must I beat him?"

"Be quiet, Bert, dear God in Heaven," said Mother. "He's had the shoes three winters now and can he help it, good God, can he help it if he grows and his feet break out at the sides?"

This seemed to anger him more than ever. Whenever Mother tried to placate him his temper only flared up higher. He burst into the bedroom and turned on the light. I sat up in bed. He was holding the shoes in one hand, and with the other he took my arm and pulled me out of bed and into the dining-room, shouting all the while that I was a lazy good-for-nothing who didn't care a hoot in hell how hard he worked all week to keep me in shoes.

Then he beat me up. My shoulders were knuckled, my face got slapped, my head was pushed against the wall a few times. He was horrible to look at too, with his tongue doubled up between his teeth like one gone mad and his eyes inflamed from beer.

Mother drew the blinds and closed the front door, pleading with him all the while. "Bert Gillady, it's late, Bert, Bert the neighbours, dear God the neighbours. Let him alone, dear God, it's late. Bert, please, please. Bert! *Please!*"

Even under that storm of knuckles and slaps nothing wet fell out of my eyes. I went to bed in a rage of stopped-up hatred and sadness, wishing for my own death or some terrible disease or disability to strike me. But I knew mine was not a growing heart and there would be no death for me.

At ten o'clock the next evening I went to spend my night of vigil. Steve was beautiful in his casket. The undertaker had combed his hair exactly as Steve had worn it in life; he had coloured his cheeks and lips with a pale carmine that made him look better than ever. It was only Steve's perfect stillness that revealed his death. The casket was lined with white satin, and Steve wore a dark blue suit. His hands were folded across his abdomen, and entwined in his fingers was a white rosary with a silver cross. At either end of the casket were tall, thick, highly ornamented candles; red flames danced on the tops of these and emitted a faintly incensed black smoke that rose like fine silk ribbons to the ceiling. There were flowers everywhere: gladioli, roses, carnations, chrysanthemums. In front of the casket was a praying bench, a bench made for knees to rest on while one said prayers for the dead and stared at the unwinking black lashes, unmoving red lips and still, still unbreathing body of Steve.

It was a long night, a pleasant one. My fellow vigilante was Steve's middle-aged uncle who sat licking his moustaches for an hour, then he fell asleep. I walked about the room touching and smelling the flowers, looking at the names signed in the guest-book of visitors who had come to express their sadness and love. I looked at the cards buried in the bouquets. In deepest sympathy from Mr. and Mrs. Kaczorowski and Bartholomew: In deepest sympathy from Auntie Marie and Uncle Nate; In deepest sympathy from Mamma and Papa Lezkoski. For a few minutes I sat looking at Steve and perhaps I slept—or maybe I was still awake—during the time I dreamed the funeral was my own. But at one time or another, waking or sleeping, I replaced Steve in the coffin.

My skin was no longer acne-cracked, I was no longer too thin or poorly dressed, and my hair was as black as Steve's with shining brilliantine waves. I was perfectly still. A roomful of people wept, and flowers engorged the room like a flood-tide. On my lips was a faint but distinct and charming smile.

In the middle of the night Dolores, unable to sleep, moved slowly down the stairs in her housecoat and slippers. She walked directly from the bottom of the stairway to Steve's coffin. She knelt on the wooden praying bench, made the sign of the cross and kissed Steve's cold cheek with her lips. Good-bye, Stevie, she said, and she began to weep. I walked over to Dolores and she threw her arms about my waist, as her father had done, and wept harder.

Late in the morning we were assembled in the living-room: Steve's family, his closest friends and relatives, the priest, Father Fulta, two altar boys, the other pallbearers and myself. I knelt near the casket at the head of which stood Father Fulta. In the back of the room near the door knelt Mr. Kurkowski, Dolores, Bernadine and Edwin, and their children. Father Fulta began to lead the final prayers, a rosary in Polish, before the body would be hauled off to the church for the funeral mass.

During the night I hadn't slept and now, in the warm room in which the air was sick with flowers and people, I was weak with tension and hunger and fatigue. The priest said the first half of the Polish Hail Maries and the congregated mourners replied. The first words of their reply, *Holy Mary Mother of God*, sounded, in Polish, like *Shonta Maria Mot-ka Boshla*. These words seemed to sing out above the others in a kind of comic chant as the chorus of voices prayed on. *Shonta Maria Mot-ka Boshla*. The rhythm of the words and their strange Slavic sounds soon created a sense of unreality as if this assemblage were taking place in a dream. Then everything began to seem funny.

How funny the way the candles flickered, the voices, the stillness, the throbbing of the room, the pompous mechanical sadness of pot-bellied Father Fulta as he led the Polish prayers, and how funny this whole ceremony of death when you think how much less pomp accompanies one's life; everything funny, even the sounds that pushed into my ears shoving the sense out, *Shonta Maria Mot-ka Boshla*, and the lightheadedness of being tired and sad and unable to cry.

Suddenly one voice which had been silent joined in with the others, a throaty burlesque male voice only a few feet to the right and behind me. *Shonta Maria Mot-ka Boshla*, said the voice in a tone so loud and deep it accompanied the others like a pipe organ. How funny it would be to watch the lips of this voice move as it rumbled out its funny Polish prayer. I glanced behind me and saw a mammoth woman with breasts the size of giant melons. She was wearing a low-necked dress and between her great breasts thick, black hair grew like jungle grass. *Shonta Maria Mot-ka Boshla*, said the voice, and the breasts heaved like great swelling hills. When I realized she was looking at me, I began to laugh. I laughed out loud and couldn't stop. Dozens of terrorized faces stared at me with reproach and shock but I could not stop laughing.

Funny everything, funny this world in which some die and others live, funny this room where everyone was uncomfortable, where all the knees were hurting from kneeling on the hard floor, funny Father Fulta who suddenly looked like Louie Armstrong.

And then his praying stopped and I heard a jazz time horn.

Father Fulta began to shake my shoulders. I fell to the floor, rolling and quivering with a laughter so deep it caused pain. Please, please stop, I pleaded with myself, think of all the sadness in the world, the starving babies in India and the cold, cold Eskimos, think of war, how sad, sad, sad and perhaps you can stop. But everything was funny, funny still. I was laughing just as Steve had laughed; it was like one of his jazz recordings in which all the drums and horns and even the piano seemed to be laughing in unison.

By now everyone was standing, staring at me in horror. Father Fulta had stopped praying and was shaking my body with his hands, *Come out of that, Boy*, he said, *Come out of it now, d'you hear, you got to stop this, Boy*, he said, and his voice was like a comic bass fiddle carrying the jazz song melody: *Come outa that, Boy, Come outa that, Boy*. I thought of the time my guinea pig had died, how I had cried then but now it had become funny, the wrinkled-up nose of the guinea pig frowning as if its sense of smell had been offended, and now Father Fulta looked like the wrinkled-up dead guinea pig.

My father's face appeared from the rear of the room. His hand landed across my face and there was no longer anything funny left in the world.

Mr. Kurkowski was kneeling by the casket now, praying and weeping. Father Fulta's hand was on his shoulder, comforting him. The assemblage was dispersed. Mother took me home and gave me breakfast. She said I was not to worry about what had happened, for it was hysteria and everyone would understand.

"Dad, too?"

"Of course."

Whenever somebody died on our street, my father and Bad-boy Billings would chip in on a quart of whisky, and they would slip it back and forth when no one was looking. My father usually carried it inside his coat and you would often see them disappearing together, Bert Gillady and Bad-boy Billings. "Go ahead, Bad-boy, you look like you could use it," my father would say with tender concern, and Billings would toss off a neat slug, wipe his mouth with the sleeve of his dress suit and hand the bottle back. After the top half of the bottle was emptied they would begin to take their mourning more seriously; no matter who it was that had died, tears might appear in my father's eyes and Billings would say: "You're takin' this thing pretty hard, Bert." My father would nod gravely and reach inside his coat.

Steve's funeral took place on a raining grey day. By the time we arrived at the cemetery my father and Bad-boy had finished their quart of whisky. The earth was muddy and at every step water oozed like black blood out of the new spring grass making your feet wet and slippery. The casket had not yet arrived and all about the freshly dug muddy grave the mourners stood with their umbrellas hoisted high and raincoats and hoods covering their bodies waiting for the arrival of the bier.

Stretched lengthwise across the grave were two long metal bars to be used as tracks for sliding the coffin over the hole. The priest began to pray in Latin. My father and Bad-boy Billings stood at the head of the grave. I heard my father whisper playfully to Billings, with an accompanying nudge in the ribs: "Careful Bad-boy, you'll fall in!" Bad-boy snickered secretively, nudged my father in appreciation of his wit, and meanwhile lost his balance. When he grasped my father's arm for support, Bert Gillady fell into the grave, feet first.

One long groan of horror rose from the group of mourners as they crowded about leaning forward to look at my father in the grave. My father's hat came flying out of the hole. He was standing now but the bald spot on top of his head was still one foot below the ground.

Bad-boy glanced quickly about him to see if there were any accusing glances and then, satisfied that no one but he, and possibly I, who didn't matter, had witnessed that unhappy nudge at Bert Gillady's ribs, began to take charge of removing my father from the excavation.

"Now keep your head, Gillady. Don't get panicky. Just take it easy and keep your head," he said. My father's bloodshot eyes looked at him with that hateful threat I knew so well. Then Bad-boy addressed the crowd. "Stand back everybody, nobody's going to get hurt. Now one of you men take hold of that steel bar, I'll get this end of it. Gillady, you get a good grip on the middle of it there. That's it. Ready now, men. Heave!"

But the steel rod was wet, my father's hands slipped away as if they had been greased with butter, and once again he disappeared into the hole.

When he looked up, lost, humiliated and frightened, everyone began to snicker silently, and then to laugh. Father Fulta tried at first to suppress his amusement but finally gave up in despair and turned away from the grave shouting hysterically in Latin.

Many of the women, in mortification from their own laughter or their husbands', and with the excuse that the rain was now too much for them to bear, ran back to their cars. When I looked at Steve's father, he seemed to have been distracted from the fact of death, and possibly even vaguely to enjoy the proceedings.

The rain fell harder. Many of the men continued in their efforts to pull my father out of the grave; but it was not until several minutes later when the casket and the cemetery workers had arrived that, finally, with ropes, they were able to pull Bert Gillady to safety.

I knew what the night would be. Mother would close the windows and upon my shoulders the weight of Bert Gillady's unhappiness would descend in his knuckles, and I would weep the long loud mechanical tears of pain.

Bert, Bert, dear God the neighbours, she would say, her eyes big with compassion, and the windows would be closed; thump slap knock thump thump slap until the humiliation was emptied from him. I knew what the night would be. The boy has princely ways, Laurie, he laughs while others cry; must I beat him? Must I whip him?

Oh Bert, Bert, *Bert, dear God!*

I knew what would happen, but now, busy with getting my father into the car, they had forgotten me. I stood alone watching the activity in the graveyard. There were people running in every direction as the casket was rolled across the steel rod tracks. Father Fulta continued the prayers and only the closest members of the family were left to attend the lowering of Steve's body into the earth.

I knew what the night would be like but it didn't matter. Steve's burial had become a magnificent event in jazz time, in which the sins of all the people concerned, even my father's, seemed to have been forgiven. There was much rain still, and it made the earth lovely; the new grass was sprayed with moisture and it gleamed under the soft white light of clouds.

Weeping in the Chinese Window

We who dwell in cities are apt to see a hundred faces or more each day, for the streetcars, drugstores, offices and elevators are filled with them. Ninety-nine times out of a hundred, the image will sift through and disappear without having made a difference in our living and doing; but when the image of a particular face lodges itself in the heart, we who dwell in cities are in for change and this is the miracle we live for.

Until this particular day in spring, then, Polly had lived her life according to a pattern, one that seemed to have designed itself: she was a bookkeeper for the real estate broker whose office was around the corner from her house, upstairs from the shoemaker's place; in the evenings she played checkers with her father or darned his socks while he read the evening paper; she visited regularly a complaining old woman, Mrs. Godspell, who was blind and lived in a house in the Mexican district. Polly would visit her bearing gifts of kindness and sweets and once a week she trimmed the old lady's hair and shaved her moustache for her. Polly made fudge for the church bazaars, she arranged the doilies on the backs of chairs, fingered knick-knacks on glass shelves and collected dolls from faraway countries. The framework of her world was the Baptist Church. It imposed certain limitations but there was a decided satisfaction to be gained from living within them. In small ways of course, one strayed. The minister, for example, had stated simply and flatly that movies were sinful, but Polly knew that a little vice adds flavour to your living, just that tiny harmless sin to keep one human.

There were others: she had been known to smoke a cigarette and in her dresser drawer, second from the bottom, you would find a small bottle of blackberry brandy. It was comforting to belong to a church whose really major sins one never had occasion to commit anyway; you could amuse yourself with venial mischief and remain holy by abstaining from that which was not even available.

On the surface she was composed, graceful. Some young people were put off by the slight hunching of her shoulders which was designed to minimize the protuberance of her breasts. This and other attitudes like blushing made them ill at ease without their understanding why. But to the older people, Mrs. Godspell, the ladies of the church, her father, to them she was a model personality, thoughtful, attentive, devout. It was as if she had, by relinquishing her claim to romantic love, spared herself the unnerving panic suffered by those who still expected it; as if she had, as a child, swallowed a thin wafer of a watch and that its mechanical unvarying tick-tock, muted by flesh, had become her heartbeat.

There were times of course, late at night mostly, when she might weep because of the stillness that had crept into her room. Her weeping was a delicate mechanism, almost anything could set it off. Now late at night a fire engine, say, will roll shrieking through the city. In her mind, the siren paints a flash of red excitement, the blaze, the action of the men, the conspiracy of flames hell-bent on eating a man's house. And when that siren and the blaze soften in the distance—what replaces it, what is sure to arrive in its wake? The silence. At such times the clock would tick like a sidewalk hammer and the ghosts of people she had passed in the streets paraded into her night-time mind. If these uninvited were too numerous or persistent, Polly would go to her dresser drawer and toss off a neat portion of the blackberry brandy.

The night was apt to be a difficult time for any human being and she did not believe it was necessarily more trying for herself than for others; think of Mrs. Godspell the blind woman whose night was eternal. Polly would send up a prayer of thanksgiving and, warmed by the brandy and the fact of an inevitable sunrise at morning, would fall asleep. More and more as the months grew into years she found herself less and less intimidated by the loneliness; it was her nature to be cheerful and the silence had become almost friendly.

Polly met Howard on a Saturday night in April. The church services had ended. Polly strolled east along the big street. It was part of the week's routine: she would stop at the bakery for what Pappa called his Sunday morning simmacooka, a bastard German way of saying coffee cake; something for the old blind woman Mrs. Godspell who made up for in sweet teeth what she lacked in vision, and if it took her fancy, something for herself.

The street was, as always, choked with a large traffic of visitors from faraway cities; it vomited eternally a curious carnival jazz made up of the voices of souvenir peddlers, newsboys, stage-whispering race-track touts and music from cocktail bars and the accordions of blind beggars. But out of street sounds rose one long cool wave of churchlike quiet from the interior of Hi Sing's Oriental Imports.

It was Polly's favourite shop. In his show window, symmetrically arranged on a square of golden cloth, lay merchandise like votive offerings to an unseen god; irregular lumps of jade mounted in silver, boxes of jasmine tea and perfumed charcoal, jewellery studded with aquamarines, pillboxes of gold embossed with black dragons. Polly, wooed by the silence, would stop here for long moments fingering with her eyes each pagan object. She would go inside to buy a miniature parasol, a paper fan, a handkerchief—but the object itself was of no importance; what Polly took away for herself was a mysterious unseen thing to which she could give no name. It was a portion of the silence, the inscrutable Oriental quiet of the shop itself.

Several months ago, Hi Sing had placed in his show window a life-size image of Buddha. It was three feet high, it sat cross-legged on a low black podium. Its face was yellow, porous, alive-looking, but in the smile was a hard impenetrable deadness.

That very day, the first time Polly laid eyes on him, she had recognized him instantly; it was like the coming together of long separated friends. A brief mutual appraisal seemed to take place. She looked through the plate glass at the Buddha: he was made of plaster, there was nothing movable inside of him, no heartbeat, no temperature fluctuation, no blood flowing. And he smiled constantly, saw everything, felt nothing.

Polly saw also her own image reflected in the glass that separated them; her skin, even-textured except for a mole on her chin from which grew several unclipped brown hairs; her eyes, close together and perpetually startled; hair clinging to her scalp like fine wire in a massive tangled knot; two glossy white teeth protruding from lips which had never been painted.

Polly seemed, even to herself, never to have been slapped or kissed. There were no scars by which one could detect past pleasures or pains. It was as if the world, in thinking her ugly, had sealed the life of her body in a kind of waxen gloss which preserved her from the marks and scars of experience that are indelible to others. And now, next to the window image of herself was this Buddha whom she had begun, in her way, covetously, to worship. She worshipped him for his calm and for his proud secret complacency. In her heart she tried to imitate his smile, his plaster-of-Paris neutrality, his freedom from desire.

But in the next block she met Howard.

A small crowd had gathered to watch the antics of a slick dollar landscape artist. He had set up his easel and stool in the window of an otherwise vacant storeroom. He began with a bare piece of canvas board and three and a half minutes later ended up with Lake Louise, complete with Rockies, in six sunny colours, all for the price of a movie. A high school girl squealed and ran inside to buy the painting. Meanwhile the spectators smiled at each other.

It happened that Polly's smile went to Howard. He was a slender black-haired young man with deeply hollow cheeks and bright eyes.

"My God, there ought to be a law," he said. "I mean that's assembly line stuff and the kid thinks it's great."

"Maybe he's just supporting himself," Polly said, "for the masterpieces."

"A guy like him? You don't believe that! I mean, Hell, he hangs on to that brush like it was a screwdriver. You think Picasso discovered cubism like this—painting a landscape in sixty seconds flat? Why this jerk wouldn't know . . . !"

The young man stopped talking. His face relaxed, he grinned wide like a child. "Hi," he said. "I'm Howard."

Polly was trapped; his voice threw her in, his smile locked the door, and I'm Howard—that transformed her dress into gossamer. From then on she was naked and in pain. She tried to walk away from him but all volition was drained. The separation would have to be his doing.

Now after Howard had said who he was and after his smile had wrapped around her like an arm, they began to walk together up the Boulevard. He was disgusted with the store-window artists, filled with contempt for all wholesalers of inferior beauty; he had to let off steam. They passed a cocktail bar where certain throbbing dizzying heights were being reached by a horn-drum-piano combination inside.

"You take jazz," he said, "those guys got more art in one finger—" He held up his little finger—"See? More art than that guy's got in his whole family for three generations back."

His voice poured over her like a narcotic bath. He was explaining jazz, how it was played for single people who were lonely; you didn't have to beat your brains out being lonely before you liked it but single people were kind of split up in a million pieces and jazz temporarily puts them together.

Jazz and the Buddha, Polly's mind ran these two together and it was as if the smile of the Eastern god had become so many chunks of dyed plaster floating through her blood stream.

"Well, that's a very interesting theory," she said, not knowing what to say. "I never thought about it quite that way. You seem to know an awful lot about it, Howard. Are you a musician?"

Then the voice began again: no, he was not much of anything though in the army he had been a bugler; he had more to say about being in the army and some of the words he used were intensely bitter ones. But Polly was not listening. Her mind and heart were in a bag slung over his shoulder. This response to the strange young man angered her; it was a deep and terrifying puzzle to have been mistress of oneself for twenty-five years and then to find that, out of a crowd, in a moment's time one had been enslaved by some sweet wizard; to find that like a child one must follow the jazz-loving pied piper as he walked along the street spewing out ordinary words, making them sound like deep honey-voiced magic from a flute.

Now they were standing in front of the bakery where the pied piper stared covetously at a lemon meringue pie. He said he'd buy it if he had a place to eat it; his landlady did not want him lugging food into the room; ants, roaches, bedbugs, you know landladies, he said.

Polly paused at the front door of her house.

"Howard, if I should happen to, without lying or anything like that, give the impression that you belonged to the Baptist Church—would that upset you?"

"Huh?"

"Pappa's sweet as a baked apple, but we're Baptists and..."

"Nuts to that, I'm going to say I'm a Yogi."

She knew that was a joke so they went inside. Her father was sleeping. She lighted a fire under the kettle. Howard wanted to smoke a cigarette and Polly hunted all through the house for a delicate cloisonné candy dish that would double for an ashtray. When she returned to the living-room he was flicking ashes into his trouser cuffs. "Oh dear," she said, "Pappa doesn't smoke, neither do I." The teakettle had begun to whistle and Howard followed her into the kitchen explaining how in cloisonné the Chinese laid the fine brass wire, a very special technique which the results hardly warranted, he said, holding up the candy dish.

Polly was busy with her fears: what if Pappa should wake up, what if the coffee were too strong for Howard;

what if he should stop talking—would she find something to say? Her hands shook and her mouth was dry.

She spread a clean plaid luncheon cloth on the breakfast nook table, taking special care to make it hang evenly on all four sides.

"Why don't you just cut it," he said, "and we'll eat it over the sink."

"Huh? Oh really? Would you rather?"

He shrugged, Polly poured the coffee, they sat down. Howard talked about the meringue, it contained some artificial preservative of which he disapproved. It seemed to her that Howard liked talking very much; it was wonderful to have so many opinions and to be positive about them, and enthusiastic. He said something that amused him and began to laugh. Polly grinned weakly and glanced at the door.

"Am I talking too loud," he said in a whisper.

"Oh! Of course not. With Pappa it's like dying when he sleeps. Why we could talk right into his ear and..."

"Now you take the human voice," Howard broke in. "Think of it. Do you know the human voice is capable of producing a wider variety of sounds than any man-made instrument?"

Polly had just deposited a lump of lemon meringue pie on her tongue when Howard's gaze settled on her mouth; there was some question in her whether or not she should swallow or talk with her mouth full. Unable to decide she sat perfectly still and did nothing.

"I mean that's something," he said; "think it over. You can scream with it, you can grunt. I mean you can moan with it, you can whimper. One instrument. And you can sing. God, it's *fab*ulous when you think about it, not to mention just laughing. Or talking."

The lump of pie sat on her tongue but Polly was too embarrassed to swallow. For a moment Howard glanced at the ceiling listening for some other sound of which the human voice was capable; during this interim she swallowed. He heard it.

"It can gulp!" he said, with a triumphal snap of the fingers. "And who knows what else. I mean you know?" Polly began to choke and she hoped he would not add that to the list. He didn't. Instead he jumped up and slapped her back. "Take some water."

"Thank you," she said, "Goodness, it went down the wrong way."

"Does your father snore, Polly?"

"What, Howard?"

"Snore?"

"I don't think he does. I just don't know if he does or not. I can find out for you."

"Of course snoring's not really the voice so much as just air coming out of your nose."

Polly was suddenly exhausted. Some absence of clear thinking had dragged her into this, one untimely exit of will when it had been most needed. She should have politely returned his smile and walked away. But she had been weak, and here was her prize: to sit trembling with the tensions of inadequacy, performing unnatural smiles and floundering for syllables until the hour was ended, until the handsome young man for whom only attractive young women were eligible, had left, until the magician had gone elsewhere with his flute.—What was it now: does her father snore? Is snoring a function of the vocal chords or of the nose? She does not know, Howard. Is trembling a function of the heart? Will it end when you walk out that door?

"Would you like more pie, Howard?"

"I'm full," he said. He did leave finally, after very little ado, after a scanty good night; after he was full, he left.

Polly turned off the porch light and, carefully avoiding the mirror in the hallway, went to her room. She undressed mechanically and quickly. With concentrated effort she was able to stifle the progress of her thoughts. Shortly after her face touched the pillow her mind began to follow Howard down the walk and into the streets, but she called it back: Jesus bless me, my sleep is for the greater honour and glory of our Father in Heaven; Amen.

The doorbell rang. She put on a housecoat, ran down the stairs and opened the door. It was Howard.

"Hey, I forgot to get your phone number and all that. I mean can I have it?"

Polly asked him to wait. In the kitchen she wrote her name and telephone number on a sheet of scratch paper and, returning to the door, handed it to him. Howard took her hand in his, and drew her through the door on to the porch. For what seemed a long time he looked into her eyes with a warm half-smile glittering under the surface of his face. Polly stared incredulously at his mouth. She lifted her hand and, like a child reaching for the moon, touched his lips with her fingers. The reality of his flesh and blood caused her to tremble.

"G'night," she said. Inside, Polly closed the door, rested her head on the strong supporting lumber of the bannister; she clung like a sailor to the rail as though the earth rocked under her, and wept.

Howard walked away with his heels striking the pavement like hammers. The moon and the stars lighted the earth with a sunlike brilliance that washed the blue streets yellow, illuminating shadows and the city's night-time mystery. He walked several blocks to the place where his car was parked. It was a strong powerful car, with grillwork and headlights shaped like the snout and eyes of some long-extinct monster. Howard brushed from its fender a piece of newspaper that had come to rest there; his movement was like a caress. He rolled back the canvas top and started the motor, racing it for a few seconds with his foot.

Soon he and the car were out on the highway, progressing through the country and the century, and Louie Armstrong played a good horn solo on the radio. Howard was proud of the power in his foot by which the car was accelerated across the great dark earth. He liked driving by night without lights and pretending to himself that he was the brain of a menacing black beast that dominated the countryside.

He stopped at the sea and looked long, deeply, into it.

There was nothing for one here but to watch and to listen: the conflict of the water with the slimy solid rocks, the earth and the sea, inherently dark, being lighted by other worlds. He could imagine the early ancestry of man slithering out of the deep, migrating landward like an army of fishtailed serpents establishing its beachhead; and Howard imagined his family, his mother and father and all the people he knew, even Polly, emerging now from the sea, flapping through the shallow places on feet like seal fins, dragging behind their tiny heads the scaled serpentine bodies; and he, in his own time, completely evolved, feeling within himself the impact of man's history and the approaching end of that long ironic struggle, began to laugh. Howard laughed aloud, for a long long time, into the sea. Then he took off all his clothes and drove, naked, back to the city.

Later, in his rooming house, he stood before the mirror, dreaming into the glass with longing and pride; he practised the boyish grin and other personal gestures he felt were becoming, he flexed, posed, paraded. His body, which held no clue to the Total Disability with which he had left the army, was neat and strong. A small leg wound and a condition they had termed psychoneurotic had left no outward scars. He fumbled in the pocket of his shirt for a small sheet of scratch paper and glued it with spit to the mirror:

Polly Heidt, Hillside 9-3311.

And then he made a promise to himself as his eyes moved more deeply inward, into the mirror, into that inverted room beyond it, an unreal room of reflection in which the beloved stood.

Before coming fully awake, Polly tried to remember where she had been but the images dissolved like drowned water colours. She opened her eyes. The room was filled with hard April Sunday light. She had a headache. Polly took from her dressing-table a hand mirror and examined her face in the uncompromising light of day, as if she sought to wash out of her eyes any of the dream roseate that might remain. There was nothing to be gained from beginning the day falsely.

Somewhere in sleep Howard's face had occurred and Polly would have liked to remember where, exactly, and why. Dreams were rare in her life and, like the dolls from foreign countries and the knick-knacks on glass shelves in the parlour, she liked to collect them. It was entertaining to dust them and to look at them on long evenings and rainy afternoons. But dreams were of no more importance than the dolls; you look at them, but you don't live by them.

She dressed for church.

It was a bright Sunday, thick with the beauty of springtime beginnings, but the town itself was a replica of yesterday.

The difference was in Polly.

Her heart was absent. It had flown away leaving in its wake a vacancy of restless air. At first she believed that with prayer and time this truant part of her would return. But in the early evening when the telephone rang, its sound filled the empty space inside of her like church bells ringing in a ghost town.

During the several weeks that followed, Polly and Howard were together often. Howard took her to the galleries and museums where he conducted wayward tours into his mind; she lost her painful self-consciousness with him, but only when he had wooed her thinking into some room it had never before visited, along blasphemous corridors where God did not seem to exist. Once he said that the human soul did not exist except on canvas and in books and in the horns of musicians. The way he said it made some horrible distorted sense that left Polly with a headache; she vowed in her heart never to see him again. But that night she finished the last of the secret brandy; her dreams were thin, gloomy, erratic, and all night long she wept so that on the next afternoon when he telephoned the strength of her vow had deserted her.

That evening they drove to the sea.

He showed her his power to control the automobile at terrifying speeds; her screams seemed to excite him, to spur him on to greater feats, and when they arrived at the beach she was trembling. A thick fog had settled over the coast and he told her that once, long ago, before the birth of man, rain had fallen on the earth for centuries at a time permitting not one ray of light or warmth from the sun to penetrate. This thought frightened Polly and she moved closer to him. Water lashed the rocky beach at the base of the palisades. He told her that the ocean's cavity was once, in the long ago when the earth was dry and hot as molten lead, a crucible which contained the hot yellow moon. She drew closer to him because he did not seem to be afraid and his calm smiling knowledge of the earth protected her.

The Bible had said God created the earth but it did not explain, as Howard attempted to, how the task had been accomplished. Once she began to say something about the book of Genesis but the words felt strange in her throat. What he knew and spoke of did not seem to come from a book, but from some mysterious primitive awareness peculiar to him in his maleness and somehow akin to his power over her and the automobile. Polly did not understand this power but she was filled with its drugging, terrifying effects.

She felt his breath on her face; the dark colour of his lips sent a chill into her. She tried to withdraw when his arms swung about her waist, enclosing her as his smile had done when they had first met. But Polly was incapable of protesting: his arms were a harbour where the ocean of trembling inside of her came to rest. He had drawn her mind away from the city where God lived and away from her tiny image of herself, into a world where authority and law were physical things.

Howard knew his power, and his smile was for himself.

He kissed her again and they drove back to the city across the grey vapour-covered earth over which giant serpents and tiny-headed monsters had once held sway.

Polly bought more brandy the next day, a larger bottle. Without its company her sleep had been clotted with gloom. Her life had not prepared her for any Howards and this soothing blackberry heat furnished strength with which to combat the night. She wanted to retreat, to retrace her steps to the moment of the fall and hide inside the image of Buddha in Hi Sing's window until the slick dollar landscape artist ran out of paint and everyone went home.

Howard. How to cope with him, the smile, the voice! and the unspoken promise of a great secret somewhere within him, a secret whose revelation might be made at any moment.

On the following Sunday morning they drove to the beach. The prospect of spending an entire afternoon next to Howard in nothing but a bathing suit, terrified her.

The sun was hot, the ocean quiet, the beach was pebbled with people. Removing her jacket caused Polly more pain than if she had peeled away skin. She felt that underneath was raw flesh or an even more naked continuation of the ugliness of her face. She half expected a mass sigh of disgust to rise up from the crowd, a general turning away and unmasking of horror. An eight-eyed family, two blankets away, focused on Polly with hushed and rapt attention as if she were a television screen.

She found, when she could steal a look at him, that Howard had undressed and lay relaxed on the sand with a yellow towel bunched up under his head. He wore brief black trunks. His body was a lean perfect taper from shoulders to toes, and it glistened with a light incandescent mahogany that seemed unreal.

"You know, I feel so damn at home," he said.

"What?"

"I mean here in the sun." He raised himself on his elbows. His biceps spread like neat leather balloons against his body. "What's with you? Afraid of a burn?" He watched for the inevitable raising of her hands to hide her already amply hidden breasts, then he lay back and closed his eyes.

Polly recognized this as one of the blind alley situations for which she must call upon a certain private mechanism of the mind to save her; she dropped her eyelids, imagined herself home in bed and that what was happening here today under God's Baptist sun was a dream which she was permitted to view quietly snug in the safe warmth of sleep. Now, dream-like, her spirit tucked in bed, she sent her body out to commit the afternoon's sins.

Her skirt dropped to the sand, she spread herself on a large towel beside Howard; her body, the majority of which was hidden by the chaste ruffles of her bathing suit or squeezed into smallness by the rubber underneath, was warmed on the underside by the heaps of sand while, above her, covering her like a kiss, the blazing medallion for which billions like herself had for centuries uncovered themselves, toyed hotly with her pores, dizzily with her senses. Its power closed her eyes.

Howard sat up.

He looked at the sea, its green shore line calm, its beach cluttered with people to whom he felt as unrelated as to a lake of minnows. People: separate units of biped animal life, come lately, these meaningless links in the unfathomable phenomenon of natural history, from a life in the sea. And he listened to their sounds; waxed paper crinkled away from sandwiches, squalling brats constructed fortresses of sand, giggled at the defeat they suffered from the devastating sea; portable radios raved about aspirin tablets and the great impending bomb; mothers and fathers warned sons and daughters of the dangers, you'll burn, you'll drown, you'll break your leg, the sand is filthy, the ocean is deep; from time to time bottles were unstoppered, cigarettes lighted, waterballs bounced, balloons burst, an aeroplane loomed low over the beach dragging a serpentine banner; BARGAINS GALORE—ANNIVERSARY SALE AT THE MAY COMPANY. Howard smiled. It was as if the sea tossed back at us our accumulated voices. Each one screamed out his role and, loudest of all, the thoughtless incomprehensible sea handed back its translation: a perpetual monotone of roaring emptiness.

He looked at Polly.

He watched the nothing, listened to the emptiness. Then a fear moved into him that froze the proud smile: a nightmarelike conviction that everyone on the beach had suddenly died, or had never, even in the beginning, possessed life. Some carnival trick played by the deep cosmic mirrors of the sun permitted an appearance of life to be maintained, but under this illusory nerve-show lay nothing but decomposition and death. Yonder roars the sea washing up a history no one can interpret. And what is our bed made of here in the sun but a hot mound of granulated sea corpses.

Here lies Polly, motionless, her ruffled belly rising and falling like a mechanical bellows.

Where was life? If not here, then where? Perhaps somewhere between here and the sun, hovering over the earth in rays undetectable by the eyes and ears and fingertips was a place reached by man for only random moments during the time of his body. Moments of life, thought Howard; we creep through a death called life, experiencing only fleeting moments of reality. Here lies me, there lies Polly, and somewhere—between here and the sun...

"Polly." He spoke her name with practised gentleness and warmth, his lips near her ear.

Polly's eyes were closed but she smiled. His voice had entered her senses like an oily silver arrow; on its head was some sweet drug that left her dizzy.

He wondered if she were awake. "Polly," he whispered, "Hey, Polly, I love you, Polly."

Polly opened her eyes and then the earth and the people, for Howard, came to life again. It was as simple as that.

They drove and they drove. Mountains on the right, ocean on the left. Sunset took place; it washed the earth in a momentary pink glow.

And then, in the evening, they drove down out of the mountains.

Polly wept.

"What you crying about?"

"I don't know."

"For Chrissake, quit it then."

She only wept harder.

"What's wrong with you?"

"I don't know, Howard, I'm ashamed. We shouldn't have..."

Then he pushed her away and started the motor. They drove down out of the mountains at a great speed but the speed no longer terrified her. Inside of her lay the strong seed of his warmth that protected her from all danger. The car radio blared out music. As they turned on to the Pacific Highway, a husky Negro voice swung out over the airways in a feverish jazz prayer.

> *Oh, He took a rib from Adam's side*
> *And gave it to 'im for a bride.*
> *Ye bones shall rise again.*

Through this song Howard smiled. But his smile was not intended for Polly. It travelled ahead of the automobile, into the night like a white gull, alone.

"Howard."

"Yeah?"

"I'm sorry."

"For what?"
"Crying."
"You love me?" he said.
"Yes."
"You still think it's wrong?"
"No."
The radio played on.
"Howard, I don't want you to think I blame..."
"Keep quiet," he said.

Ah knows it brothah, Ah knows it brothah,
Ye bones shall ri-ise ag'in.

Suddenly the headlights illuminated a group of approaching bicycles, their young riders dressed in white shirts. Howard pressed the accelerator and released the wheel. The car swerved toward them briefly, then straightened its course. The cyclists rushed to the side of the road, some of them fell to the asphalt, others collided. Polly screamed, the radio played on, Howard laughed.

The car stopped in front of her house.
"Howard, I..."
He reached in front of her and pulled down the door handle. The door swung open.
"G'night," he said.
She looked incredulously at his eyes which at that moment were like glossy agates stuck into an empty grinning mask, a mask that disguised nothing.

For the next few days Polly remained in bed. She lay listening to a good number of inconsequential sounds and watching the peach-coloured walls as they shrank. After several days the image behind her tears had faded, leaving a ghost whose features were blurred, indistinguishable. It was during this entertainment, this shadow show of icy remembered kisses and black over-with caresses, that Polly thought of hurling herself from a bridge or emptying a cartridge into her mouth, but at these moments she numbed herself with brandy until the temptation had passed from her.

Soon all of the pain was gone from her and she took up the habits of her former life, her visits to Mrs. Godspell, her walks along the avenue, her long pauses before the image of Buddha in Hi Sing's window. Often she would walk away from the Buddha with a puzzled frown between her eyes, and now and then she would look at a person without seeing him or run head-on into a telephone pole or a stranger in the street. But no one seemed to notice.